# LET ME KILL YOU, SWEETHEART!

# BOOKS BY FLETCHER FLORA

*Blow Hot, Blow Cold*

*Desperate Asylum (*aka *Whisper of Love)*

*Hildegarde Withers Makes the Scene* (with Stuart Palmer)

*Killing Cousins*

*Leave Her To Hell*

*Let Me Kill You, Sweetheart*

*Lysistrata*

*Most Likely To Love*

*Park Avenue Tramp*

*Skuldoggery*

*Strange Sisters*

*Take Me Home*

*The Brass Bed*

*The Devil's Cook*

*The Hot Shot*

*The Irrepressible Peccadillo*

*The Seducer (*aka *Campus Woman)*

*Wake Up With a Stranger*

*Whispers of the Flesh*

# LET ME KILL YOU, SWEETHEART!

## FLETCHER FLORA

*Special Edition*
*Featuring 2 Bonus Stories!*

**WILDSIDE PRESS**

Published by Wildside Press LLC.
www.wildsidebooks.com

# CONTENTS

# CHAPTER 1

Late in the summer of the year in which Avis Pisano was murdered in the fall, there were three young men from Rutherford who stayed for short periods at different times at the lake resort where Avis worked as a waitress. Avis was a pretty girl but not very bright. The three young men were bright enough but not on the surface exceptional. The lake resort, called Sylvan Green, was not exceptional either. It consisted of the small hotel in which Avis worked and a dozen cabins scattered among the trees along the shore. From Rutherford to Sylvan Green was about two hundred miles. Rutherford was a small town, a railroad division point, and it was even less exceptional than Sylvan Green.

Besides living in Rutherford and going that summer to the same resort, the three young men had three significant things in common:

In the first place, they were all determined, each for his own reasons, to marry the same girl;

In the second place, and in spite of the first, they all went to bed with Avis Pisano, who was extremely enthusiastic about making love;

In the third place, they were all called Curly at times by people who knew them well. In the cases of two of the young men, the nickname was applied because it was a fair description of the character of their hair. In the case of the third, by the kind of suitability one finds in calling a fat man Skinny and a skinny man Fatty, the nickname was applied because it was an exact opposite description of his hair, which was straight and cropped close.

In addition to these significant things which these three young men of Rutherford had in common, there was another significant thing, which they did *not* have in common.

One of them had murdered Avis Pisano.

He murdered her in November, about a week before Thanksgiving, and he had made love to her in the preceding July, three days before August. Immediately after loving her and long before murdering her, he lay and listened to the summer night, and he could hear many sounds. He could hear the breathing of the girl beside him, and he could hear the lapping of the water of the lake outside, and he could hear an owl mourning among the trees on the lake's shore, and he could hear the voices of a man and a woman in a boat on the water, and he could hear over and under and beyond all these the thousands of tiny unidentifiable sounds in a kind of integrated whole that was the total sound of the night.

It was hot in the little cabin. He could feel the perspiration gather in the hair in his armpits and trickle down across his flesh onto the damp sheet on the bed. The perspiration seemed scalding hot, though it actually wasn't. But it stank. He could smell his own body, and he could smell the body of the girl. The two bodies, his and hers, were hot and adherent at points of contact. In the violation of his normal fastidiousness, he felt for himself a deep disgust that was almost nauseous. For the girl, the easy conquest, he felt intense contempt. He had cultivated her with contempt and taken her with contempt, and the contempt in satiety was swollen and gross. Rolling over abruptly, he lay on his side with his back to her.

At first it had seemed amusing enough, an interlude of no consequence, and it had begun without any particular intent. As a matter of fact, now in the hot night, he could not remember how it had begun exactly, the first significant word or look that had initiated everything that was to follow. Her name was Avis, and she was a waitress in the dining room of the small hotel up the slope, a pretty girl with long legs and a long, calculating look, and it was apparent to him in the beginning of their relationship, while it was still casual, that she considered him much more significant materially than he actually was, that she was weighing concessions against possible profits. This had amused him, being so exorbitantly evaluated, and he had slyly contributed with small lies to the perpetuation of her mistake,. It served her right for being so transparently calculating, the damned little fool, but he had been conscious tonight, a little while ago in the time of the ultimate intimacy, that the element of calculation seemed to be gone from her. He was surprised and alarmed and a little sickened by the honest intensity of her immediate response, and it was all so adherent and hot and fetid, and all, in the end, so goddamned easy.

The breathing of the girl Avis was softer and smoother now, punctuated at intervals with little sounds like whimpers. The whimpering sounds caused him to remember the coarse moans she had made in her orgiastic excitement, and remembrance made him nauseated again, and even as he remembered and was nauseated, she reached out and touched his hair and trailed her fingers down his back.

"Curly," she whispered. "Sweet Curly."

He had acquired the nickname as a boy, and he had never resented the use of it by anyone before, but now he resented it fiercely, and he wished he had not told her about it. Perhaps it was because of the way she spoke it, with a kind of plea in the whisper, as if she were begging him to be kind and tender and to go on making love to her. It was bad enough to have become involved with her in a tangle of perspiring passion, and to touch her now or to commit himself to tenderness in the aftermath would be utterly intolerable. He thought all at once of the girl he wanted to marry, and he had in the instant an irrational and terrifying feeling that she was standing beside them in the darkness of the small hot room and had been standing there from the beginning to witness with revulsion his carnal performance. With terror came anger for the girl responsible, the girl beside him in the sticky bed, and the terror would have been multiplied and the anger deadlier if he had known then, as he did not, that she had played the percentages once too often and had lost. To remove himself from her entreating fingers, he rolled off the bed and stood up in the darkness beside it.

"What's the matter?" Avis Pisano said.

"Nothing," he said. "I thought I'd have a cigarette, that's all."

"Light one for me, too, and come back."

He lit a cigarette and handed it to her, but he did not light one for himself nor resume his place beside her. He walked across the room to a window and looked out across the lake. The moon cast upon it a silver shadow of light. Beyond the window the night air stirred and crept inside to dry his body and cool its fever. Behind him from the bed, he could smell the smoke of the cigarette and hear the long whispers of breath that expelled it from her lungs.

"Come back," she said. "Please come back."

"It's too hot," he said. "It's cooler here by the window." He wished she would go. He wished she would get up and dress and go away and that he might never see her again or remember again what they had done. Anger and impatience must have edged his words, for she did not speak for a full minute, and when she did speak again, it was again with the suggestion of pleading in her voice.

"You're angry," she said. "What have I done to make you angry?"

"I'm not angry. As I said. I only want to stand here by the window for a while."

"Didn't I please you? Is that why you are angry?"

"Goddamn it, I am not angry. Why must you keep insisting that I am?"

Her bald reference to their intimacy revolted him and increased the anger that he denied. Now that they were finished, why in hell couldn't she simply get up and go away and leave him alone? He could feel her behind him in the bed, staring at his back through the darkness and trying to decide in her rather dull mind what it was that she had done to offend him. As a matter of fact, he did not know precisely himself, for she had only been agreeable and ardent in a function to which she was obviously no stranger, and now afterward it was certain that she wanted only a little consideration and tenderness in return. It was merely a casual relationship, cheap and sordid but no more, and there was surely no rational reason for his feeling that he had somehow imperiled himself, that he had in the last half hour started everything going wrong that had before been going so beautifully right.

"If you're worried," she said, "you needn't be. I don't expect anything from you."

"Of course not. I didn't imagine that you did."

He forced himself to turn away from the window and approach the bed. He took her cigarette from her fingers and crushed it in a tray. Proceeding now under a compulsion to go ahead with whatever was necessary to get the whole business finished with as little emotion as possible, he sat down beside her and began to stroke her shoulders and forearms with his hands.

"I'm sorry," he said. "Honestly, it's only that it's so hot in here."

"That's all right. I just didn't want you to spoil everything."

She sighed and began to breathe unevenly again. Feeling the response of her flesh to his fingers, he stood up abruptly.

"Why don't we go outside and walk along the lake for a while?" he said.

"Do you want to?"

"Yes. It will be much cooler there."

"All right. I'll go if you want to."

She got up and began to dress, and he sat down again on the edge of the bed and lit a cigarette and kept his eyes averted.

He thought that he would go away in the morning. He would get up early and go away.

# CHAPTER 2

The conductor did not see Avis Pisano when she boarded the train, but later, when he went through her car checking tickets, he noticed her particularly because he thought she looked ill.

It was cold in the coach in which she rode. Huddled in her seat with her cheap fur coat pulled closely about her, she shivered and stared through the window at the gray countryside slipping drearily past under a dull steel sky. Ordinarily, her face would have been prettier than most faces are, but now it was livid and lax and gave an effect of pathetic futility to the cosmetics that tried to brighten it. She looked very tired as well as ill and her lips were stretched tight on her teeth and turned down at the corners in an expression of ugly bitterness.

She presented her ticket without speaking, and he punched it and went on about his duties, but a long time later, when he came through the car again, she looked up at him and said, "How long will it be before we reach Rutherford?"

He stopped and consulted his massive silver watch. Looking down at her, thinking again that she looked really quite ill, he felt for her a thin but genuine compassion that did not disturb him greatly but was sufficient to lift her in his mind above the gray, collective anonymity of his other passengers.

"We're due in fifty-five minutes," he said.

"Thank you."

She began looking again at the back of the seat ahead of her, seeming as she did so to shrivel and grow smaller inside the cheap fur coat, and he remained for a moment looking down at her, unconsciously replacing the massive silver watch in its assigned pocket to complete a routine action that had become long ago the ritual of his peculiar dedication.

"Are you all right?" he said.

"Yes, thank you."

"Well, it won't be long now. Just fifty-five minutes to Rutherford."

He moved on down the aisle and out of the coach and did not return until forty minutes later when the train was stopping at the last station before Rutherford. The train ground to a halt through a series of diminishing jerks. Through her window, the girl was looking down upon the rough, red brick of a small platform washed with watery yellow light, and the conductor also looked out past the reflection of her impaired face in the glass. A man passed along the platform, pulling behind him a four-wheeled baggage truck on which there was no baggage. The man was dressed in striped overalls and a short, blue, heavy jacket. On his head was a black-and-red plaid cap with flaps turned down over his ears. The train started again with another series of jerks, gathering momentum as it labored into the night.

"Rutherford in fifteen minutes," the conductor said.

Avis Pisano glanced up and down. "Thank you," she said.

Fifteen minutes later when the train stopped finally at Rutherford the conductor was standing on the station platform as Avis descended from the car with the assistance of the porter. It was very cold on the platform, the wind sweeping across from north to south, between the station and the tracks. The station was really quite large for a small town, because Rutherford was a division point. The center section of the building, smoke stone and stucco, was obviously the main waiting room. North of the waiting room in the same structure was the baggage room. South of the waiting room was a restaurant with steamed-over windows. Standing just outside the entrance to the restaurant, leaning back with his shoulders braced against the wall of the building, was a man in a too-short topcoat that reached not quite to his knees. He looked across at the girl Avis, the only passenger to descend from the train, with what seemed mild curiosity, and she, the conductor noticed, seemed to be looking with a kind of quiet desperation for someone who should have met her but apparently hadn't. Then, following the direction of her gaze down the length of the platform into the darkness beyond the reach of the yellow light, he saw dimly, as she did, the shifting and separation of a shadow, the lifting of an arm in a gesture of beckoning.

Carrying her bag, she hurried down the wind in response.

# CHAPTER 3

It was no later than half-past-six when Purvy Stubbs went down to the station to watch the seven-o-five come in from the north. It wasn't much of a train, only a local and hardly worth watching, but to Purvy a train was a train, and any one you cared to mention was worth watching any time you cared to choose. This was because trains were in his head and blood.

Something is always getting in someone's head and blood and this can be good or bad, depending upon circumstances. If it's something a person can do something about, quite a bit can frequently be made of it. Beethoven did this with music, for instance, and Van Gogh with painting. On the other hand, if it's something a person can't take advantage of, it's very likely to become eventually a bitterness and a frustration. Thereafter, everything the person does in his life, no matter how commendable, will be to him of little importance simply because it seems so insignificant compared with whatever it was that had got into his head and blood earlier to torment him all his days. There was a poem written about a fellow in this condition. His name was Miniver Cheevy, and he was miserable.

With Purvy Stubbs, it was trains. As a kid, Purvy was shy and awkward, and he never grew out of it, but he had remarkable things in his head. Besides the trains, that is. Among these remarkable things were little scraps of poetry about this and that. These scraps of poetry were all delicate little bits of pretty sound, and you'd have thought that merely saying them aloud would have shattered them completely. Not that Purvy often said them aloud. They were just there in his head with the trains, left over from the reading he'd done, and every now and then with the proper association one or another of them would get into his consciousness and he'd think about it for a while.

It's impossible to say just how and when the trains got into Purvy's head but he was certainly very young when it happened. This in itself was nothing unusual for lots of kids like trains and plan to be engineers when they grow up. In most cases they change their minds and become farmers or grocers or doctors or something else, and there is no trauma in the change at all. It's just that wanting to be an engineer is something they grow out of painlessly. It's not even very unusual when a kid wants to be an engineer and actually grows up to be one. It's often done and is a satisfaction to both the kids and the people who own railroads. What made Purvy's case different and rather sad was that he could never accomplish either of these two alternatives. He never got to be an engineer and he never quit wanting. He stayed shy and he stayed awkward, and the trains stayed right in his head.

He was born and had lived all his life in the town of Rutherford. Except for being a division point on the railroad, Rutherford was not much of a town, and no matter where you lived in it, you were not far from the tracks. You could hear the long sad sound of whistles at all hours of the day and night, and possibly this was the way the trains got into Purvy's head in the beginning. Possibly they got into his head through his ears, for the whistling of a train is a seductive sound, and it is a sound that would quite likely stick around in the kind of head that was inclined to retain scraps of poetry and things of that sort.

Purvy's devotion to trains made his Old Man wild. The Old Man was president of the Rutherford Commercial Bank, and he was determined that Purvy was going to be president after him. For a long time he was as patient as he could be with Purvy's deviation, thinking that it was just kid stuff that Purvy would grow out of in good time, but as Purvy grew older he only seemed to become more and more set in his deviant devotion. He slipped off to the station to meet every train that he possibly could, sometimes cutting classes at school to do it, and at the sound of a whistle he'd quiver like an old hound scenting game. Old Man Stubbs privately wondered if he'd given issue to some kind of unclassified maniac, and as time went on and Purvy got worse instead of better, he very nearly lost all patience entirely.

The situation broke wide open the summer after Purvy graduated from high school. One day he went into his Old Man's office at the bank, and it was pretty apparent immediately that he had screwed up his nerve and had come to get something off his chest.

"Well, Dad," he said, "I want to tell you that I've decided to take a job with the railroad and try to work my way up to being an engineer."

The Old Man just sat and looked across his desk at Purvy for a few seconds, and then he stood up and walked over to the door of the office and closed it quietly. After that, he turned and gave Purvy a terrific kick in the ass. It was a kind of sneak attack, and Purvy wasn't braced for it. It catapulted him into a chair, and he fell sprawling all the way to the floor. Rolling over, he sat up on the floor and kept sitting there for a while, looking up at his Old Man as if he couldn't believe what had happened to him.

"Well, Purvy," his Old Man said quietly, "I'm bound to tell you that you aren't going to do any such thing, and if there's one thing I'm determined about, it's that there isn't going to be any goddamned engineer jockey in the Stubbs family. What you'll do, you'll either go off to college in the fall like a reasonable person, or you'll come into the bank and work like a dog until you know the banking business inside out You have a choice of either one of these two prospects, and that's all the choice you have, and if I hear any more hocus pocus about working for the railroad, I'll kick your ass up and down Main Street."

Purvy stood up slowly and rubbed his bruised butt.

"I'm not going to college," he said. "I'm sure as hell certain of that."

"All right," his Old Man said. "Then you'll come to work in the bank, and you can count on it."

That's what Purvy did. He went to work in the bank. The truth is, he was a nice big lubber, but he didn't have the guts to face up to his Old Man over an issue. He didn't learn much about banking, however, because he wasn't particularly bright and didn't have his heart in it, and he never got the trains out of his head. Now that there was no hope of his ever becoming an engineer, the trains took on for him a kind of bittersweet, antebellum-like quality that made them more seductive than ever. Whenever he went to the station and saw an engineer bringing in one of the big steam jobs or a diesel, he felt like a fellow thinking of someone else in bed with a girl he wanted to be in bed with himself. He learned to hate his Old Man in a quiet way that never showed, and every single chance he got, he went to the station to watch the trains. He knew the time schedule of arrivals and departure by heart, and if his Old Man didn't watch him like a hawk, he was apt to walk right out of the bank during business hours. After business hours, unless a most critical contingency prevented it, you could depend on his being at the station for every train without exception, excluding only the few that passed while he was sleeping. He was almost always pretty early, and he was early this night, as has been said, the night that Avis Pisano came to Rutherford.

He went first into the warm waiting room and saw by the large electric clock above the ticket agent's window that he had fully thirty-five minutes to wait. Then he went into the men's toilet and relieved himself. It was like that in cold weather, it seemed. He had to relieve himself much oftener than was necessary in warmer seasons. Coming out of the toilet, he stood and looked slowly around the waiting room, feeling for the hard oak benches something that was very much like reverence, as if they were pews in a chapel, listening with a rather sorrowful contentment to the friendly staccato sound of the telegraph in the ticket agent's office. There was no one in the room except himself and an old man in a ragged black overcoat who was asleep in a sitting position on one of the benches. The old man's jaws, surmounting sleep, worked slowly and rhythmically at a cud of tobacco. Beside his feet on the floor was a squat brass cuspidor. Seeing the cuspidor, Purvy thought suddenly of one of those little scraps of poetry that were always moving in and out of his head according to associations.

*A bright bowl of brass is beautiful to the Lord*, he thought.

He held the scrap in his head for a minute and then let it go. Crossing the waiting room, his too-short topcoat flapping around his knees, he went out onto the windy brick platform beyond which the parallel pairs of steel tracks lay shining in yellow light to the edge of darkness. The wind sliced through his clothing and threatened to tear his hat from his head. Turning his back to it, he went down to the entrance of the restaurant in the south end of the depot. Inside, the warmth was as sudden and almost as shocking as the cold had been on the platform. It was a steamy kind of warmth, heavy with the rich aroma of hot coffee. There was an oval counter in the middle of the room with stools all around the circumference, and inside the oval, the only other person present when Purvy entered, was the waitress, Phoebe Keeley. She was pouring water into one of a pair of polished coffee urns.

Purvy sat down on one of the stools at the counter and said, "Hello, Pheeb."

Phoebe finished pouring the water into the urn and replaced the cap. When she was finished, she smoothed her starched white uniform over her broad hips and walked slowly, with a swaying of the hips, down to where Purvy was sitting. She was a big girl, easily five-ten in the flat heeled shoes she wore to work in, and she carried quite a bit of weight even for so much height. It was firm weight, however, nothing flabby, and satisfactorily distributed. Beneath thick blond hair done in a bun on her neck, her face was broad and not pretty, but it possessed, nevertheless, a heavy attractiveness that was somehow primitive in its effect. As a matter of fact, the total effect that Phoebe created was so substantial that it seemed tangible, something that could be touched and contained in the hands and turned over and over for inspection. A lot of the fellows around Rutherford thought Phoebe would be really something to have, and a couple could have testified to the truth of it, but Purvy wasn't one of them and wasn't likely to be. He was too busy thinking about trains.

"Hello, Purvy," Phoebe said. "Come down to see the seven-o-five in?"

"That's right."

"You want a cup of coffee?"

"I wouldn't mind."

Phoebe returned to the urns and drew a cup and brought it back. Purvy watched her broad hips going and coming under the white uniform, but he didn't get the pleasure out of it that most fellows would have got. He stuck his nose into the steam rising from the coffee and took a couple of long sniffs.

"Smells good, Pheeb," he said. "Thanks a lot."

He didn't offer to pay for it, because it was understood that it wasn't expected. Free coffee was a kind of tribute to his long devotion to the trains. Sometimes he bought a sandwich or a couple of doughnuts or something of the sort, and for these he was expected to pay, but never for coffee.

"Is it getting colder outside?" Phoebe asked.

"It's pretty cold. The wind's come up."

"Well, it's about time for it, I guess. Almost Thanksgiving."

"You're right, at that. Next Thursday. Time sure gets away, doesn't it, Pheeb? It only seems like a little while ago that it was Thanksgiving last year."

"Oh, I don't know. Seems to me that time usually drags in this dump. I get awfully damned bored sometimes."

"Dump? Rutherford, you mean? Rutherford isn't so bad, Pheeb. There are lots of worse places than Rutherford."

"All I can say is, I'd hate like hell to live in a worse one. I wonder why it's always on Thursday. Thanksgiving, that is. Did the Pilgrims start it or something?"

"Hell, no, Pheeb. The Pilgrims didn't start it at all. Not as a regular holiday, anyhow. Lincoln started it with a proclamation right after the Civil War or sometime around then."

"Is that a fact? I thought the Pilgrims started it."

"Well, they didn't. They didn't have a damn thing to do with it. Not as a regular holiday."

She stared at him silently for a moment, shaking her head slowly from side to side.

"You're an odd ball, Purvy," she said.

Purvy looked surprised, almost shocked, as if it were entirely beyond his understanding that anyone would consider him in any way unusual.

"Me? What's so odd about me?"

"Well, take those lousy trains for instance. Why are you always hanging around to watch the lousy trains come in and go out?"

"I like trains. Ever since I can remember, I've liked trains. When I was a kid I wanted to be an engineer. I wanted to be an engineer more than anything else in the world."

"Why didn't you be one, then? It seems to me that almost anyone could be an engineer."

"My Old Man wouldn't let me. He made me go into the bank."

"How the hell could he make you go into the bank if you didn't want to?"

Purvy thought about this for quite a while, as if he were wondering himself, for the first time in ten long years, just how his Old Man had managed it.

"I don't really know," he said. "I just sort of gave up on the trains and went into the bank like he wanted."

"Well, I'll be damned! Did you tell him how *much* you wanted to be an engineer?"

"Sure. I told him, all right."

"What did he say?"

"To tell the truth, he didn't say anything right off. First thing he did, he kicked my ass. He kicked it so hard I fell over a chair and landed on the floor. Then he told me I couldn't be an engineer and would have to go into the bank, and I went."

"I'd be ashamed to admit it, if I were you. Damned if I wouldn't. A great big lubber letting his Old Man kick his ass and boss him around like a baby. Not that I'm ready to say he was wrong. Personally, I can't see why anyone who could work in a bank and maybe someday be president of it would want to be a crummy engineer."

"People aren't alike," Purvy said. "It's all a matter of how you feel about different things."

He drank some of his coffee, listening already for the first sound of the whistle of the seven-o-five, and Phoebe looked at him and started shaking her head again.

"I'll bet you're lonely," she said, a note of surprise in her voice, as if this were a sudden flash of insight, a kind of revelation.

"I guess everyone is lonely sometimes," he said.

"What you need is to forget these goddamned trains and how you wanted to be an engineer and go find yourself a nice girl. A fellow whose Old Man is president of a bank could find all kinds of interesting girls if he wanted to."

"I don't think so," Purvy said. "I've never much liked girls to tell the truth."

"Oh, crap, Purvy. A girl with anything on the ball could *make* you like her. I'll bet I could make you like me plenty if I took the notion. Besides, I heard you been going to Phyllis Bagby's every once in a while, and that doesn't sound to me like a fellow who doesn't like girls. The way I get it, you've got to like Phyllis about twenty dollars worth before she'll give you any time at all."

"Well, Phyllis isn't exactly a girl. She's thirty-five, thirty-six if she's a day, and I only go there once in a while to talk."

"*Talk*! You go to Phyllis Bagby's to *talk*? Purvy, you're a big liar, that's what you are."

"It's the truth, just the same," Purvy said, "whether you believe it or not."

"Well, you can bet I don't believe it," Phoebe said, "unless talk is a new word for what fellows go to Phyllis Bagby's for." At that moment, two men came in from the platform and sat on stools at the oval, and Phoebe departed to wait on them. Left alone, Purvy began to think, now that Pheeb had brought her up, of Phyllis Bagby. The way Pheeb had referred to her, you'd think Phyllis was a common whore or something, but that wasn't true. It was a long way from being true. The truth was, Phyllis didn't have anything at all for sale except the services of her nice beauty parlor on Main Street, and those were for women, naturally, and she took in more than enough money from the beauty parlor alone and had no need whatever to supplement her income from other activities. The reason Phyllis had a kind of reputation around town, the kind just intimated by Pheeb, was because she was a real looker who made you think of a regular professional model or something, being a beauty operator and knowing just how to accomplish it. She liked men and wanted them, but she didn't want them around her neck. Anything she gave them or got from them she was given and gained in free exchange, without commitments from either side. She was a widow whose husband had died young in an automobile accident out on the highway, and she had a nice brick house on Locust Street with a colored girl to take care of it. The colored girl's name was Lutie, and when you went to the house in the evening, Lutie was sometimes there to let you in, if you were let in at all, but afterward she went off and was not seen again.

It was a joke how Purvy got acquainted with Phyllis. It happened one night when Purvy was especially depressed from thinking about how the only life he would ever have was being misspent in a bank while fine big steamers and diesels were running free on the rails of the American continent. As a consequence, he was hating his Old Man with even more intensity than usual and was unconsciously wanting to get even for everything by doing something he knew his Old Man would disapprove of. Dropping into the taproom of the Division Hotel, he drank a couple of beers and got to talking with Guy Butler, who was drinking bourbon in water and had been at it for quite a while before Purvy arrived.

Guy was a dark, thin-faced fellow with a bitter mouth and a crippled left hand. The hand had been smashed up in the war almost twelve years before, when Guy was just barely twenty, and it was a particular misfortune in his case because he had been a kind of genius at playing the fiddle, a child prodigy, and had already, before the war, been a soloist a couple of times with the philharmonic orchestra up in the city. When he had returned from the war with the smashed hand, the one he fingered the fiddle with, he had tried to learn to play all over again with his left, but it hadn't worked out. He had tried desperately and for a long time, in a sort of feverish agony, and often in the middle of the night, if you passed the house he lived in with his folks, you could hear him working and working and working and getting slowly a little better. As a matter of fact, he got damn good, but damn good is not good enough for someone who has been superb, and one afternoon he walked into the living room of his house and quietly laid his fiddle and bow on the fire in the fireplace, and that was the end of it. His mother was there having some tea with a couple of ladies at the time, and after Guy had put the fiddle and bow on the fire and walked out, she sat and watched them burn and began to cry silently with the tears rolling down her face.

Purvy liked Guy. He liked him and felt sorry for him and was of the opinion that they had quite a bit in common because of the fiddle in Guy's case and the trains in his. He had to admit, though, that Guy's trouble had distorted his personality to some extent. Ordinarily he was friendly and kind and generous, but sometimes, when he got to floating his bitterness in bourbon, he became cruel. It was as if he were slashing out in retaliation at anyone handy, and that's the way it was the night he sent Purvy to Phyllis's. It was a cruel kind of joke on Purvy and Phyllis both, either one of whom would have given almost anything in the world to make Guy's hand good again.

Talking with Guy in the taproom, Purvy couldn't help letting his depression show, and he even said a few hard things about his Old Man, which was something he seldom did. He thought them frequently, but he seldom said them. Guy listened silently, staring into his bourbon and water with a twist to his thin lips, and after a while he looked up at Purvy with a shine in his dark eyes that should have been sufficient to warn Purvy to back off.

"What you need," he said, "is to go see Phyllis Bagby."

"Phyllis Bagby?" Purvy said. "What good would that do?"

"You'll be surprised at the good Phyl can do you. The least you can do, anyhow, is to give her a chance. I'm always going to see Phyl when I need pepping up."

Purvy had heard a few of the things that were said about Phyllis, of course, and it crossed his mind right then that his going to see her would be something that would infuriate his Old Man. Tomorrow he would remark rather casually that he had been around to Phyllis's, and then he would have the pleasure of listening to the Old Man fume and call him names. Once it had disturbed him to be called things like a bum and a fat, lubberly fool by his Old Man, but it didn't disturb him any longer, and in fact it gave him pleasure because he had come to understand that the names applied to him as a defective son were a reflection in consanguinity upon the father, and that this reflection was also understood and detested by the Old Man. For this reason, the Old Man's vulnerability to his own abuse, the idea of going to Phyllis Bagby's appealed to Purvy, but he was afraid that it wouldn't work out. Actually, he was simply afraid, period. Phyllis was a damn attractive woman with a smooth sophistication about her, downright beautiful in Purvy's eyes, and therefore formidable. He was afraid of all women, except his mother and a few elderly relatives and maybe Pheeb Keeley at the depot restaurant, and he was particularly afraid, because of his awareness of his own homeliness, of beautiful women. Moreover, the area of his fear was excessively enlarged by the fact that he considered any woman who was even vaguely pretty to be beautiful. Now, entertaining Guy's suggestion, he simply couldn't believe that Phyllis would have anything whatever to do with him, and she might even have him hauled in by a cop for trying to molest her or something.

"I wouldn't have the nerve to go," he said.

"Why not?"

"I don't know anything about women to tell the truth."

"Anything you need to know, Phyllis can teach you. Phyllis is the greatest little teacher you could hope to find."

"Well, she's so beautiful and sophisticated and everything. She must have all kinds of men who want to go to see her, and it isn't like that she'd have anything to do with me."

"Oh, hell. You walk in and lay twenty bucks on the table and she'll have something to do with you, all right."

"Really? No kidding, Guy?"

"Sure. Why the hell should I kid you? It's nothing to me if you go or not."

"I know, but Phyllis has her beauty parlor and makes plenty of money, and I can't understand why she'd have to do anything like that on the side."

"Don't ask me. Maybe she gives it to charity."

"Anyhow," Purvy said, "I couldn't do it. I just haven't got the nerve."

Guy shrugged and finished his bourbon and water and went away. Purvy stayed at the bar and had another beer, and after that, without quite knowing precisely when or how the decision was made, he found himself outside walking toward the street Phyllis Bagby lived on. When he reached her house, he hung around on the front walk for quite a while, his decision wavering, but finally he hurried up in a moment of resolution and rang the doorbell. Lutie wasn't on duty that night, and Phyllis herself answered the bell. She was dressed in a brown woolen dress that looked expensive, simple and perfectly fitted, and she smiled at Purvy in a friendly way. "Hello," she said.

He said hello and stood there awkwardly in the light from inside as she looked him up and down.

"Well?" she said.

"Guy Butler said I should come," he said.

"Guy? Come for what?"

"Well, he just suggested it. You know."

"I'm afraid I don't." She smiled at him, and the smile was still friendly. "You're Purvy Stubbs, aren't you?"

"Yes, I am. That's who I am, all right."

"Maybe you'd better come in and explain. Would you like to come in?"

"Yes, I would. Thank you very much."

He went in, and she closed the door after him. The living room of the brick house was conservatively and comfortably furnished, softly lighted, and there was a fire in a brick fireplace at the far end of the room. He stood just inside the door, turning his hat around and around in his hands, and after a moment she took the hat with a little laugh and tossed it into a chair.

"You seem to be upset about something," she said. "Maybe it would help if you'd just tell me directly what it is you want. It might make you feel better."

He didn't know how to tell her. As a matter of fact, he was wishing desperately that he hadn't been such a fool as to act upon Guy's suggestion. Maybe Phyllis sold it, but she surely didn't look or act like someone who did, and he had an uneasy feeling, in excess of the unease he would have felt in any event, that he was in an extremely precarious position. Suddenly, with an imperious compulsion to get it settled one way or another, he walked forward to a small table at the end of a sofa and laid a twenty dollar bill on it. Then he stood looking at it, feeling like more of a lubberly fool than his Old Man had ever said, and Phyllis stood looking at it too. After a while she said softly, "What's that for?"

"You know," he said. "To pay."

He didn't have the nerve to look at her, and it was a good thing that he didn't, for she had gone deathly white with fury, and it would have terrified him if he'd seen the way she looked at that moment. However, she could see very well that Guy had duped him, and she felt sorry for him, and in the end the compassion transcended the fury. She walked past him and picked up the twenty and handed it back to him.

"Put it in your pocket," she said. "Go back and tell Guy Butler never to come to my house again so long as he lives. Tell him never to speak to me or look at me or suggest in any way that we are in the same world."

That was enough for Purvy. Even he was capable of understanding then that Guy had played a wicked joke on him, one of those cruel things Guy would do when bitterness and bourbon collaborated. He took the twenty, still without looking at Phyllis, and turned and started stumbling across to the door. He was almost there when Phyllis spoke again.

"Wait a minute," she said.

He stopped, standing with his back to her, waiting.

"Don't tell him that," she said. "I'd be sorry if Guy never came again. He can't help being cruel now and then, and we must both forgive him. You and I. Tomorrow he'll be sorry and will come to tell me so."

He agreed with her, knowing Guy, but was unable to say it. He swallowed painfully and remained silent.

"If you knew him as I do," she said, "you'd know I'm telling the truth."

"I know him pretty well," he said, "and I know it's true. I won't hold it against Guy, but I'm sorry I did what I did."

"Well, never mind, so long as you understand."

Before he could think better of it, because it got into his head so suddenly, he said, "*All places shall be hell that are not heaven.*"

"What?" she said.

"Nothing. It's something someone wrote. I was thinking how it kind of fits Guy. Sometimes, anyhow. When he's feeling particularly bad and does things like this. He can't ever be what he wants, and he knows he can't be, and so nothing else is any good at all, and it's like being in hell, and he does things to people."

"You're right. It certainly fits him." She paused, looking at his broad back. "Maybe there are times when it fits all of us. Tell me, Purvy, would you like to stay a while?"

After she said that, he had the nerve to turn and look at her. He could see plainly that she wasn't angry, more sad than anything else, and he smiled at her sheepishly.

"If you don't mind," he said.

"All right. Come and sit with me in front of the fire, and we'll talk."

They sat there for quite a long time, a couple of hours all told, and he told her about the trains and his frustration and his quiet hatred for his Old Man, and afterward he felt remarkably relieved and good, and inexpressibly happy that he'd come, even though it had meant showing, in the beginning, what a fool he was. During the two hours. Phyllis had three calls on the telephone, and it was apparent from the way she talked that at least two of them were from men who wanted dates, and she turned them down, and it made him very proud that she should do this for him. The truth was she truly liked him, and she felt sorry for him because he was an ineffectual fellow with a simple dream that was already dead, and this made her feel warm and generous toward him. A generous and kindly woman by nature, when Phyllis felt sorry for someone the extent of her generosity was incredible.

At last she said, "What you came for. You really didn't want it, did you?"

"I don't think so," he said.

She laughed. "I really didn't think you did. Even in the beginning. I don't know whether to feel respected or scorned."

"It's not you," he said, getting red in the face. "It's me."

"Why did you come in the first place, really?"

"I don't know. I guess I thought it was something my Old Man wouldn't like, and that's why."

"I see. Well, anyhow, I hope you haven't been disappointed."

"Oh, no. It was fine talking to you."

"Thanks. When you feel like talking again, give me another try."

"I'll do that. You bet I will."

And he did. Sometimes it was possible for her to see him, and sometimes it was not possible, and sometimes he went and stayed all evening, and sometimes he went and stayed for a little while and left when someone else came later, but in the beginning and always afterward there was nothing between them but talk, and this was the simple truth whether Pheeb Keeley or anyone else believed it or not. It was one of the good things in his life, a partial compensation for the abortive and still-born engineer.

*The whistle. The seven-o-five.*

Hearing faintly the sorrowful, seductive sound, he got off the stool in the restaurant and hurried outside, taking up a position on the cold platform beside the door. The laboring local puffed in and stopped, blowing off steam as if it were panting with exhaustion. The porter and the conductor came down the steps from one of the coaches and stood waiting. Soon a single passenger, a young woman, appeared at the top of the steps and handed down her bag. She followed it herself and stood beside it on the platform. In her cheap fur coat, she seemed, somehow, abandoned and wretched and on the verge of a definitive defeat. Suddenly, after looking down the platform toward the south, she picked up her bag and moved quickly in that direction.

Turning his head to follow her progress with, mild curiosity, Purvy saw for an instant in the darkness beyond the platform a shadowy figure that receded and disappeared. In the instant that he saw it, there was something that struggled for recognition, a vague familiarity of shape or size or distinctive motion, but then it faded as the figure faded and could not later be recalled.

# CHAPTER 4

Curly stood and waited in the cold darkness and cursed the winter and the remembrance of summer. He had left his car parked near the tracks almost two blocks away in a place where the odds were great that it would not be seen and had walked up along the tracks to his present position in the darkness at the south end of the station platform. He was standing in a very small park, an aesthetic effort to relieve the raw ugliness that was natural to the environment of a railroad yard the grass dead under his feet but the surrounding upright and Pfitzer Junipers living and green and rustling in the wind that swept down across the platform from the north. Near him in the little park was a stone bench, but it was too cold to sit down. He stood well back from the edge of yellow light, waiting for a train and a girl on it, and he wished with all his strength that the train would wreck, pile up in a mass of distorted steel, and that the girl would die swiftly in the cold night and be out of his life forever.

He remembered the summer and cursed it. He remembered the fool he had been in the summer, and he cursed the fool. It had been late summer, really, almost the end of July, and he had gone by himself to this small resort called Sylvan Green. Two weeks were all he had for a vacation, besides being all that he could afford, and he had intended to spend them quietly in fishing and loafing and, most of all, in making plans for a girl named Lauren Haig, cool and golden and wanted. He had already made a remarkably careful study of this girl before going to Sylvan Green, and he had cataloged precisely and exploited deliberately her vulnerabilities, which were many, and he was certain at last that she was in love with him and almost ready to do whatever he asked, but now it was all in jeopardy, the entire precise and beautiful conquest, because of a cheap little bitch in a summer resort who was had too easily.

He had left Sylvan Green the morning after the consummating night in the hot little cabin, and it was not until quite some time later that he had received in Rutherford the first of the notes. And that was the beginning of fear and hate and the threat of ruin, his precise and beautiful plans in sudden jeopardy, and it was all the result—oh, damn, damn, damn the cursed luck!—of a cheap little glandular episode at a third-rate little resort with a rotten little bitch who was at this moment coming through the night in a train to ruin him utterly.

The last of the notes had come that afternoon, and it had been lying on the table in the hall when he got home in the evening. With a rising feeling of sickness, he had recognized it immediately for what it was. The pastel envelope whose pretensions could not hide its cheapness. The cramped, childish script on the front of it. The absurd green ink with which she always wrote. He had picked it up and carried it upstairs with him to his room. In previous notes, exactly three of them, there had been nothing more than entreaty, a desperate supplication that he had known how to appease without explicit concession or denial. Reading this one, he had been struck by its quality of bitter determination, the expression of a decision reached in a manifestation of unsuspected strength.

*You must help me*, she had written. *It's the least you can do, and you've got to do it. I won't listen to any more lies or anything, because I know very well you've been lying to me, and I'm coming to see you on the train that will arrive in Rutherford at five minutes after seven Saturday evening. I hope you will meet me, but if you don't I will go to a hotel and make you see me later. I'm not mad or anything, and I know everything is as much my fault as yours, but none of that makes any difference now, and it's just that I need help, and you've got to help me. If you don't do it willingly, I'll go to a lawyer or someone like that and make you, and I will also go to this girl you say you want to marry and tell her all about it and maybe spoil everything for you. I'm sorry this happened, and I'm sorry I have to be this way about it, but it's partly your fault because you don't seem to want to help me.*

That was all, and it had terrified him. And after the terror had come an interval of icy fury. Tearing the note and the envelope into fragments, he had sat on the edge of his bed and pounded a fist into a palm and cursed her to hell in a whispered monotone for what must have been five full minutes. Following the fury and the cursing was the final phrase of his adjustment to the emergency, and hour or more of calm, almost impersonal calculation that had pleased him greatly as a sign of his own immense potential and had filled him with a kind of singing sense of dark immeasurable power. In that hour he decided that the simple and complete resolution of his difficulty was for Avis Pisano to die.

Now, suddenly from far down the tracks, came the whistle of the seven-o-five. Almost immediately, within seconds, the door of the restaurant in the depot opened, and Purvy Stubbs came out and stood waiting on the platform with his shoulders braced against the wall of the building. Unconsciously, though it wasn't necessary, Curly shrank back a little into the darkness of the park. It was imperative, of course, that he not be seen.

It was absolutely imperative that he never be significantly connected in anyone's mind with the girl on the train who was going to die. Watching Purvy, that lubberly, lonely man at his incredible devotions in the coal-smoked chapel of his dead, ridiculous gods, Curly smiled with derision, feeling in the uplifting magnitude of his own design a cold contempt for lesser destinies and commitments.

The train had come into the station now and stopped. Avis descended from her coach and stood alone on the platform, and he was gratified to discover, now that the necessity of her dying was established, that he was able to look at her with practically no emotion whatever, neither anger nor fear nor even futile regret. Aware all at once that she was looking directly at him down the lighted length of the platform, he stepped forward three paces and raised an arm and stepped quickly back again in shadows. But she had seen him. Lifting her bag from the platform at her feet, she hurried toward him.

In the dark little park among the rustling Junipers, she stopped and set her bag on the dead grass and said tiredly, "Hello, Curly."

"Hello, Avis," he said evenly.

"Are you angry with me?"

"No. Not at all. I'm not at all angry."

"I thought you might be. I dare say I'd be, if I were in your place."

"I'm not angry, but you shouldn't have come here. I told you not to come."

"I'm sick and frightened, Curly. I don't know what to do, and I had to come. I couldn't help it."

"I suppose so. Does anyone know you came to see me? Have you told anyone who you are?"

"No. I didn't think you'd want me to. Honestly, Curly, I don't want to cause trouble, but you've got to help me. You've simply got to."

"All right. Anyhow, there's no use standing here in the cold. Come on. I've got a car parked down here by the tracks."

They walked south along the tracks to his car, and if she wondered why he had left it in such a distant and secluded place, she asked no questions. Perhaps she was by then too tired and ill to wonder about anything, or too relieved that he had come to meet her at all. After they had walked a short way, she placed a hand on his arm to steady herself, and he could feel her trembling.

The distance he had driven to the station had not been sufficient to start warm air coming through the heater, and it was very cold in the car. He put her into the front seat, and she sat huddled against the door, hugging her coat about her. Getting in on the other side, he could hear her teeth chattering. He started the engine and drove away parallel to the tracks, turning right at the first crossing.

"You're going away from town," she said. "Where are you taking me?"

"Only for a drive. It will give us a chance to talk."

"I'm very tired. I want to go to a hotel."

"I'll take you to a hotel soon."

"I'm cold. I think I'm going to be sick."

"We'll have some warm air in a minute. It won't take long."

He continued to drive west on the street, and in ten minutes they had reached the edge of town and turned south on a farm-to-market road. After the turn, he reached down and switched on the heater, and the small fan began to hum and force warm air into the interior of the car. Avis sighed and let her head fall back against the seat, and he could almost feel in his own flesh and bones the sudden, sensuous relaxing of her tired body. After a minute, when the warmth had increased, she turned her head and looked at him with dry, entreating eyes. She opened her coat and he saw she wore a short sleeveless evening dress. She saw with a queer little catch of pain that was not related to parasitic life the fine line of his boyish profile touched and softened by the tiny lights on the dash. Her evaluation of masculine appeal was still basically adolescent, substantially as superficial as it had been ten or fifteen years ago, and seeing him now and feeling the pain, she succumbed at once to the same emotion that had already made her a fool and had destroyed vague plans and was now threatening to destroy her life.

Impulsively, she said, "Do you remember the night in the cabin? Do you ever think of it?"

He turned his head to look at her quickly, immediately looking away again. Remember? He remembered, all right. Good Christ, the remembrance made him sick to his stomach. The hot adherence, the soft swift surrender, the utter idiocy that had put everything he really wanted in its present peril.

"How could I forget?" he said. "It's the reason we're in all this trouble, isn't it?"

"Yes," she said tiredly, "I guess it is."

They had now traveled several miles down the graveled road and had not passed a single car. Suddenly, scarcely decreasing their speed, he turned left, east, and descended a grade on a frozen dirt road, crossing at the bottom a stone culvert that spanned a dry slough. Beyond the culvert, he pulled over onto the shoulder of the road and stopped. Turning off the lights but leaving the engine idling to continue the heat, he twisted on the seat to face her.

"Now," he said.

"What?"

"Now let's talk. You want to settle this, don't you?"

"I want you to help me, that's all."

"How? Tell me how I can help you."

She raised her eyes, still dry and entreating, and lowered them again.

"The simplest way would be to marry me. I don't suppose you'd consider marrying me?"

"No. It's impossible. I've explained all that to you."

"I know. The other girl you're in love with."

"That's right."

"Then you must give me some money."

"I've already given you some."

"A hundred dollars."

"It was all I had."

"Just the same, it wasn't enough. A hundred dollars doesn't go very far."

"Maybe I can give you some more later. How much will you need?"

"I've been thinking about it, and I've decided that I ought to have at least a thousand."

"A thousand! Goddamn it, where would I get a thousand dollars?"

"You could borrow it. You could get it from a bank or something."

"Don't be insane. Banks don't loan that much money without some kind of security. Besides, how could I explain what I wanted it for?"

"I don't know. I'm not clever about such things, but I'm sure you could think of something if you really wanted to."

"I can't do it, and that's that. Why should you need so much?"

"Well, I won't be able to work for quite a while, and there will be the doctor and the hospital, and I'll have to have something for the baby."

"You needn't worry about that. There are plenty of places that take unwanted babies. Homes and places like that where they hold them for adoption."

"I'm going to keep it."

"Oh, Jesus! Have you lost your mind completely?"

"No. I've thought and thought about it, and I'm going to keep it."

"How can you possibly take care of it?"

"I'll work. I won't be the first woman who's taken care of a child by herself."

"What if you have trouble? You might get sick or lose your job or something like that. Will you expect me to go on helping forever?"

"Not unless it's absolutely necessary. I promise you that. But if it's necessary, I'll expect it. It's your responsibility too, and you can't deny it. It's only right that you should help if it's necessary."

Up to that moment, there may have still existed for her some hope of living. Afterward, there was none at all. He could see very clearly that she was an impossible fool and that she would be a menace, or at best a burden, so long as she lived. She seemed perversely determined to ruin him, and even if he could buy a reprieve now with something less than she demanded, there was no assurance at all that it would be more than that, any more than a reprieve, and she would probably return later with her miserable little bastard to destroy everything that he might accomplish in the meanwhile. Lauren and all that Lauren entailed, the beautiful precise plans. This was suddenly a terrible certainty in his mind, and he was shaken again by the fury that had succeeded the terror in his room. Slowly, with his right hand, he removed the blue nylon scarf that he wore under the collar of his topcoat.

"It's getting too hot in here," he said.

"Do you think so? I don't. I was so terribly cold. I don't think I've ever been colder in my life."

He watched her closely, twisting and twisting the scarf in his hands, transforming it slowly into a long, tough cord. "Are you tired?"

"Yes. I'm tired and I need something to eat."

"Would you like to go to a hotel now?"

"Yes."

"You're not looking very well. Do you feel as if you were going to be sick to your stomach?"

"No. Not now. I feel better than I did on the train."

"I thought you might like to get out and breathe some fresh air before we start back."

"I don't think so. Thank you, just the same."

She slumped down a little farther on the seat, resting her head on the back drawing her almost bare legs up under her and closing her eyes with a long sigh that had almost the sound of a whimper. Then, with the cold purpose that followed his fury, he leaned toward her swiftly and slipped the twisted scarf around her neck and jerked it tight.

And in the end, though she struggled some and tried a little to live, she died with such readiness that she may have accepted it, after all, as a reasonable solution to everything.

# CHAPTER 5

The town of Rutherford rises gently east of its tracks to the minor eminence of a kind of low ridge, and to this ridge, perhaps as a symbol of their social position in relation to the rest of the population, Rutherford's rich withdrew to build their homes. It is not a very long ridge, but it does not need to be, for the rich in Rutherford are few, and so, consequently, are the homes of the rich. The homes are all built on the same side of the concrete street that runs down the ridge's spine, all facing the town that sprawls below, and affording from the rear a bucolic view of the valley beyond. The view of the town is quite pretty at night, when darkness hides the scars and brings out the lights, and the view of the valley is even prettier in the day with its scattered red and white farm buildings and multicolored parallelograms of crops and grass and turned earth, and so the privileged inhabitants of the ridge are not deprived at any hour of something charming to look at.

Among the big rich houses, the biggest and richest by quite a bit was the house of Gordon Haig. There are many places, of course, where it would not have seemed so much, but in Rutherford it seemed like very much indeed, and it was. It was natural and proper that Gordon Haig should have had the biggest and richest house by quite a bit, for he was by quite a bit the biggest and richest man. Unlike most of the other wealthy or at least prosperous men of Rutherford, he was not associated with the railroad. He owned a shirt factory that provided employment for nearly a hundred people, and he was actually a millionaire, which was something that no one in Rutherford was. It was rumored that he was worth about five million dollars, but this was not true. He was really worth a little over one million, which was plenty, and he had in addition to all those dollars and the accumulation of things that dollars bring, a wife, who does not count, and a daughter who does. The daughter's name was Lauren, and she was pretty.

The night that Avis Pisano came to Rutherford on the seven-o-five and was murdered, Lauren was sitting alone in her room in the biggest, richest house on the ridge. She was sitting there when the train came in, and she was still sitting there several minutes later when Avis and Curly were driving west out of town. She was sitting in her panties and bra and was doing nothing, which was something, if nothing can be something, that she did quite often. She was a tall girl with hair almost precisely the color of the valley parallelograms in which wheat had been planted and stood ready to harvest, and she had a beautiful willowy body that she herself admired in a narcissistic sort of way but hadn't made much use of. She was twenty-six years old and single. The reason she was single, in spite of being attractive and rich, was not because she had lacked chances, but simply she had never in her life been able to take a definitive step about anything important, and marriage is certainly a definitive step, if nothing else. This night, the Saturday before the Thursday that would be Thanksgiving, she was thinking about this, about marriage, and about three young men of Rutherford who wanted to marry her.

*Rex*, she thought.

*Ellis*, she thought.

*Guy*, she thought.

*Rex or Ellis or Guy*, she thought.

Of the three images that the three names invoked, one elicited a stronger response, a warming and stirring of the blood in her body, and of this one she began to think exclusively. Remembering his voice and the trespassing of his hands, she felt in remembrance an itch of desire that was as close to passion as she ever came. Passion had always seemed to her a kind of degradation, impossible in herself and ugly in others, the acts that incited it being violations, and she could not understand how this one person, this one young man of Rutherford, could cause her to feel as she had never felt before and had never wanted to feel. She did not understand it, but at last she accepted it. When he called her darling and stroked her body, or even when she thought of it after the time, as she now thought of it in her room this Saturday night, she felt submissive, if not responsive, and she was certain then, with only the slightest uncertainty afterward, that he was the one she wanted and would marry. When they were married, they would live in a fine house that her father would build, and she would reign coolly and quietly among expensive and gracious accoutrements that her father would buy, fabrics and silver and shining crystal, and perhaps now and then, only occasionally, there would be the times of desire and necessary submission.

*Curly*, she thought, *Oh, Curly*, giving him in her mind the warmth of affection his warm, affectionate name.

She had, as a matter of fact, a date with him at eight o'clock, and it was surely getting late, pretty close to the time, and it was necessary to get up and begin dressing if she was to be ready when he came. Looking at the electric clock on the small table beside her bed, she saw that she had indeed been sitting and doing nothing—unless you counted thinking, which was, after all, a kind of doing—for much longer than she had thought, and that she would have to hurry now to make up the lost time.

Standing, she went into the bathroom and turned on the shower, adjusting the flow of hot and cold water until she had the proportion precisely as she liked it, just slightly less than intolerably hot. She would have much preferred a bath to the shower, but the shower was quicker and must therefore be had in concession to time, or the lack of it, and she kept reminding herself while she was having it that it was time to stop and get on with her dressing, but it was very pleasant under the hot stinging spray, almost as pleasant as it would have been to lie in the tub, and she remained there, as she had remained sitting previously in the bedroom, much longer than she intended.

Out of the shower and dried at last, she returned to the bedroom and began selecting the clothes she would wear, and she was conscious all the while of the pressure of time and the necessity to hurry, and she actually thought that she was conforming to the necessity, but it was only the consciousness of the pressure that made her think so, and really she did not hurry at all. Before beginning to dress, holding the first sheer trifle in her hand, she stopped for a moment to consider herself, to feel the cool, aesthetic pleasure she had in sole possession, and she thought sadly, with a kind of abortive nostalgia, that this would be lost when she was married, or at least it would be impaired, and she would never again belong to herself in quite the same way that she now did. But she understood that this was a way of thinking and feeling that was bad for her and that must be abandoned once and for all for her own good, and so she began deliberately to think again of Curly, of Curly's voice and Curly's hands, and she began at the same time actually to hurry at last. Telling herself that he would surely arrive at any moment, and might even be in the house already, though no one had come to tell her so, she finished dressing and went downstairs into the living room, but he wasn't there yet, after all her unnecessary concern, and it was then almost ten minutes past eight.

There was no one in the living room but her, and there seemed to be no one but her in the whole house. At any rate, though she stood quietly and listened intently, she could hear no sound, and the house had suddenly the feel of an empty house. She remembered then that her mother and father had driven up to the city and would not be back until morning at the earliest, but there should be servants in the house, the maid and the cook, and she wondered where they were. Going back into the hall into which the stairs descended, she walked past the stairs to the rear of the hall, and then she could hear, beyond a closed door to the kitchen, the sound of movement and after a few seconds the sound of one voice saying something followed by the sound of another voice saying something else in reply. Relieved to learn that she was not alone in the house, but not quite knowing why she was or should have been, she returned to the living room, and it was by then a quarter past the hour, and she was a little angry. This was foolish too, however, as foolish as having been disturbed by the empty feeling of the house, and if Curly was a little late, if he had been delayed for one reason or another, it was certainly nothing to get upset or angry about, and what she would do, since it was necessary to wait, was watch television or listen to some music. She would listen to the music, that's what she would do, because music was something you could select and play according to your own taste, while television had to be taken as it came and could be pretty awful, which it almost invariably was.

At the record cabinet, she read through the index of recordings, which was on a card fastened to the inside of the cabinet door. She did not want anything too somber, nor did she feel in the mood for anything that was, on the other hand, particularly gay, and so she finally selected Tchaikovsky's *Pathetique*, which was both. The part she especially liked and wanted to hear was the second movement in 5/4 time, the strange and haunting rhythm that seemed to her a kind of deviation or distortion, and the movement had just ended and been succeeded by the march-scherzo when the front door bell sounded in the hall. Leaving the recording playing, she went out into the hall and intercepted the maid, who was coming up from the kitchen.

"I'll get it, Martha," she said.

The maid stopped and turned and retreated to the kitchen, and Lauren went on to the front door and opened it, and it was, as she expected, Curly at last. His face had assumed already, when she opened the door, a small-boy smile of contrition and entreaty. "I'm late," he said, "but I have a good reason. Really I have. Do you forgive me?"

"Of course," she said. "It doesn't matter in the least. I was playing some music and hardly noticed. It's quite safe for you to come in."

He laughed and came into the hall and removed his coat. "Well, please don't be *too* indifferent. I think it would be more flattering if you were a little angry."

"All right. At first I was a little angry, but now I'm happy. Is that satisfactory?"

"Would you object to showing me how happy you are?"

"Not in the least. I admit that I've been anticipating it." She put her arms around his neck and raised her face, which was something that always required in the very beginning an inner effort, a small conquest of reluctance, but then he was kissing her, and his hands were on her body, and she felt the familiar quickening of blood that was now accepted and even wanted, and in the living room the march-scherzo came to an end and was followed after a moment of silence by a swelling symphonic cry of deepest sorrow, *Adagio lamentoso.*

He raised his head abruptly in an attitude of listening, and she felt in his body a sudden rigidity. Looking up across the set, flat planes and almost classic projections of his face, she saw a shadow across his eyes that seemed in that instant to be a shadow of the music itself, as if sound had substance that could block the light. He was staring over her head into the room from which the music came, and it was perfectly apparent that he had been caught and fixed and profoundly affected, and she wondered mildly why this should be so, but it was easily understandable, after all, for it was surely profoundly affecting music.

"What is that?" he said. "What are you playing?"

"It's the *Pathetique*," she said. "The last movement."

He gave a sigh, a prolonged whisper of released breath, and his body shivered and grew still as rigidity left it. "It's a dismal thing, isn't it?"

"It is, rather. Do you want me to stop it?"

"No, no. Let it play out."

"I put it on in the first place only to hear the second movement. The 5/4 part, you know. Someone said once that it's like a waltz for a three-legged man. I admit that it's very queer, but I like it."

He laughed again and kissed her again, and the music ended in the second kiss as it had begun in the first, and afterward they went into the living room, and the night went on from there.

The night grew a little older, and after a while, after quite a while, in the softest of light that was hardly more than a shadow of light, she submitted to the subtle, persuasive hands and the strong, seductive word said softly and softly and softly again, *darling, darling, darling.* And she would then have agreed to anything he asked. He could then have done with her whatever he chose.

But he couldn't be sure, and now in his delicate and precarious game he would certainly be the greatest of fools to risk by imprudence what he had sustained by murder. And so, thinking so, he attempted less than he could have accomplished, and he left early.

It was, when he left, exactly ten-thirty.

# CHAPTER 6

An hour later, at eleven-thirty, the taproom of the Division Hotel was almost deserted. The only persons present were Bernie Juggins, the bartender, and Purvy Stubbs. Purvy sat on a stool and stared moodily into half a glass of Miller's High Life that was going flat. He hadn't drunk from the glass for quite a long time, and it looked like he sure as hell was never going to drink from it again, and for all Bernie could tell from looking at him, the fat bastard might be dead. Bernie wished he would drink his goddamned beer and go home, that's what Bernie wished, because then he could put out the lights real quick, before anyone else drifted in, and beat the lousy closing hour by a good thirty minutes. A guy got tired tending bar. Tending bar was long hours and hell on the feet, and if some slob like old Purvy didn't have a damn thing to do but play dead on a stool with a glass of flat beer under his nose, that didn't mean that some other guy like Bernie didn't have anything else to do, either. He had a home, Bernie did, and in the home was a bed, and in the bed was a wife, and he could think of just a hell of a lot of things he'd rather be doing than what he was, but there was no use thinking about that now, about his wife or sleeping or anything else, because here came Guy Butler, and it was just too damn late to beat the last thirty minutes, as he'd hoped, thanks to that damn Purvy, the big dope.

Guy crawled onto the stool next to Purvy, and Bernie drifted along behind the bar and stopped opposite him. He was a damn nice fellow, as a matter of fact, in spite of hanging around in the taproom until the very last lousy minute and keeping a guy from getting a little break once in a while, and if he was a mean son of a bitch sometimes, it was something you could understand, because of what had happened to his hand and all, and you couldn't blame him a hell of a lot. Still, he certainly could do some mean things if the notion struck him. Like the time he'd told old stupid Purvy that Phyllis Bagby was a whore and had sent Purvy around to Phyllis's house with twenty bucks to buy a piece. That was mean to Purvy, and it was even meaner to Phyllis, because Phyllis really liked Guy, better than anyone else in the world, which was something everyone knew perfectly well, and she was ready any old time to sleep with him or marry him or do anything he wanted anytime he wanted to do it. That was all finished now, though, Bernie supposed, since Guy had started going out with that rich bitch on the ridge, that snotty Lauren Haig, and it sure as hell looked like Guy was deadly serious about it, it sure did, even including orange blossoms and all that crap. You couldn't blame him, of course, because the bitch would be coming into a million bucks at least when her old man and old lady died, besides being a real fancy looker that no guy in his right mind would feel inclined to kick out of bed, but you couldn't tell how it was going to come out in the end, because Guy didn't have any clear track with her like he had with Phyllis, and Rex Tye and Ellis Kuder were working at it just as much as he was and just as hard. What Bernie secretly hoped, which he admitted freely to himself, was that she'd pop off and marry someone else entirely, none of the three, and he thought it would be a hell of a good belly laugh and just what they had coming.

"What's it gonna be, Guy?" Bernie said.

"Straight bourbon," Guy said.

Bernie set up a double-shot glass and poured in a jigger of Jim Beam, which was what he always used if the customer didn't specify, and Guy took it and downed it with a little shudder and pushed it back for the same. While Bernie was pouring the second time, Guy turned to Purvy.

"How's it going, Purvy?" he said.

Purvy roused from the dead and shifted his eyes with a grin from the flat beer to Guy's face.

"All right, Guy," he said. "Can't complain too much. How's it with you?"

"Well, I'll get by as long as Bernie's bourbon holds out. You been out to see Phyllis lately?"

"I go out there now and then. Matter of fact, I was there tonight for an hour or so. Between the seven-o-five and the ten-twenty. Phyllis was asking about you. She's wondering where the hell you been keeping yourself."

"I've just given up, that's all. When you started seeing Phyllis, I quit. I knew damn well I didn't have a chance any longer with you in the picture, so I just quit."

"Oh, damn it, Guy, cut out that crap. You know damn well that Phyllis hasn't got any time for anyone else when you're around. She feels real bad because you been staying away, she really does. You ought to go out and see her."

"Well," Guy said, "to hell with it."

He picked up the double-shot glass and drank from it, a single quick gulp, but this time he downed only half the whiskey instead of all of it, and he used his left hand to lift the glass and to hold it afterward, the crippled one, but it didn't really look so bad, in spite of the scars, only a little stiff, with the fingers drawn down in the slightest suggestion of a claw when they were relaxed. The fingers were long and slender and sensitive, the kind of fingers that could draw the soul out of a fiddle, and maybe out of a woman. The reason he used the hand for everything, like eating and drinking and everything, was because it was a kind of habit left over from the days when he used it and exercised it constantly in the hope of getting it perfectly flexible again, as it had been before being hurt, and now that he'd given up the hope and had no purpose, he still did it as a kind of habit. In the opinion of Bernie, though, there was something more to it than that. Bernie liked to study people and try to figure out why they did things, and Bernie figured that Guy was deliberately throwing the hand in your face, so to speak, as a kind of bitter gesture or something—as a kind of epitaph, when you came to think of it, as if he were saying in his own special way, *Here lies Guy Butler*.

Well, Bernie thought, he was an odd son of a bitch, pretty twisted and fouled up inside, but you had to like him in spite of that, and you had a lot of sympathy for him too, not so much for what had happened to him, because a lousy bunged-up hand wasn't such a hell of a tragedy in itself after all, but because of what he had lost because of what had happened, which was something else again and a hell of a lot more. He'd been on his way to being something really big, not just fat and prosperous like old man Haig up on the ridge, who made shirts and was a millionaire, but who hadn't ever been heard of except right around close, or by the people who bought and sold his lousy shirts. Guy had been on his way to being famous and admired all over the country and in Europe and all such places, and then his hand got loused the way it was, and Uncle Sugar said thanks and dropped a pension on him, and it was over, just all over and done and nowheres to go. Well, hell, you felt a lot of sympathy for a guy like that, but you didn't tell him so, of course, because he'd spit in your eye if you did, and you liked him and wished it hadn't happened to him, but at the same time you wished it didn't sometimes make him quite so goddamned mean, either.

For instance, telling old lubberly Purvy just now that he'd quit going out to Phyllis Bagby's because he knew he didn't have any more chance after Purvy started going. That was just a way of breaking it off in Purvy for being a fellow that no sensible woman would take seriously, and it was pretty damn mean and nasty, even if Purvy was just naturally the kind of fellow you were constantly tempted to break it off in. You just absolutely couldn't understand why Purvy didn't do something about himself, though God only knew what it was he could do, running all the time to the depot to watch the lousy trains come in and go out, and it was common knowledge around town that he'd wanted to be an engineer, but his old man had kicked his ass and wouldn't let him. Look at him now. Just look at him. Sitting there like a sack of something on the stool, and just looking and looking into his flat beer as if there were a naked female swimming around in it or something. Why the hell didn't he go home like a sensible person? And why the hell didn't Guy Butler go home, too? It was a quarter to twelve now and time that everyone was going the hell home, including Bernie Huggins, who was damn well ready.

At that moment in Bernie's weary reflections, Ellis Kuder came into the taproom from the lobby and crossed to the bar, and Bernie took an angry swipe at the mahogany with his rag and watched him sourly as he got onto a stool beside Guy. He didn't like Ellis very well under the best of circumstances, and he liked him less than ever at this moment, the arrogant bastard, blowing in this way at a quarter to twelve as if he owned the crummy joint and never thinking or caring a damn that somebody might want to close up and go home. He didn't know exactly why he didn't like Ellis, when you came right down to it, and he'd tried to figure it out to his own satisfaction, because there's always a reason for everything, of course, and it's sort of comforting to know what it is, but all he could figure in the end, no matter how hard he tried, was that he didn't like Ellis very much simply because there was something about him that you couldn't like very much. It wasn't just that he was good-looking and conceited, which he certainly was, and maybe it was just a feeling he gave you that didn't have anything to do apparently with the way he looked and the things he said and did. It was a rather uneasy feeling, really, though it seemed pretty silly to feel uneasy about a guy you'd known forever, and what it was, it was a feeling that Ellis didn't care a damn bit more about you, or anyone else on earth except himself, than he cared about a horsefly or a cockroach or any kind of low life you cared to mention. You got this feeling in spite of his always being perfectly pleasant and friendly and everything, and that was the reason you didn't like him, as nearly as you could figure it.

"Hi, Guy," Ellis said. "How's it going, Purvy?"

Purvy looked up from whatever he saw in the beer, the naked female or something, and grinned without saying anything. Guy grunted and lifted the double-shot glass and drained off what was left in it. Ellis turned to Bernie, who had come up opposite.

"Thought I'd have one before I go home, Bernie," he said. "Have I got time?"

"You got ten, fifteen minutes," Bernie said.

"That's enough," Ellis said. "Rye and water."

"Same again for me," Guy said.

Purvy said nothing and Bernie poured. From the lobby, Rex Tye came into the taproom.

Well, here it was, Bernie thought, the final, culminating, absolutely last goddamned straw. No one but precious Rex himself, Mother's fair-haired boy in the flesh, and out all by himself at damn near midnight, too, and patronizing a nasty taproom where hard liquors were served, to make it worse, and keeping honest bartenders out of bed until all hours to make it as bad as it could get. A stinking spoiled brat, that's what he was, if you wanted Bernie Huggins' opinion. Even if he was a grown man. If you were a spoiled brat at ten, you were a spoiled brat at twenty or thirty or forty or any age you got to be, and that's the way it worked out. To give the devil his due, though, you had to admit that it was his mother's fault. Everyone in town knew how she'd always treated him like God and taught him that he was different from other people and a hell of a lot better, the other kids and later the other men, and the wonder was, to tell the truth, that he hadn't turned out to be a bigger stinker than he had. It was unhealthy, that's what it was, the way the damn woman hung onto him and tried to make him out to be something that he plainly wasn't, except in her own mind, and you wondered what kind of enormous ego or something she had, to keep it up that way all these years without getting wise to how phony she was and how phony she had made her brat, especially when she was as poor as Job's turkey and had to keep paying on back bills all the time, a little to one or two creditors this month and a little to one or two others next month, so she and precious Rex could keep on living like refined and cultured people and all that crap. It was like one of these lousy Freudian messes you heard about, mother and son all loused up with each other and stuff like that, and no girl had ever been good enough for precious Rex until he got after Lauren Haig, up on the ridge, and that was a horse of another color and perfectly all right, of course, because the daughter of a millionaire was good enough for anyone, even Rex, and if the truth were known, Bernie was willing to lay odds, Mother herself had probably been planning the whole thing for years, and had sicced Rex on when she thought the time was right and was goosing him along for all he was worth.

And speaking of Lauren Haig, or thinking of her, Bernie realized all of a sudden that all the competition was present, lined up at the bar at ten minutes to twelve like three night birds, with Purvy Stubbs thrown in for good measure, as a kind of extra or neutral, and it was pretty damn funny when you thought of it like that. Lined up there just like the best of cronies, the three guys who were trying to crawl into little old Lauren's bed and bankbook, and it really was funny, a real belly laugh, to see them acting like little gentlemen when they were probably trying to figure out a way to cut each other's throat. You couldn't exactly call it a triangle, like they were always making movies about, because you had to count Lauren as one of the points, which made four, and what it was, it was a regular goddamned rectangle or something. Bernie wondered which one would win out in the end, or if maybe it would be someone else entirely, which he hoped. He wondered if any one of them was maybe getting a little in advance from old Lauren, something on account, but he bet none of them was. He bet not a damn one of them was even getting a feel.

"You got eight, ten minutes," he said to Rex. "What'll it be?"

"Whiskey sour," Rex said.

He leaned forward over the bar and looked down the line to his right and said names in order.

"Ellis," he said. "Guy. Purvy."

Two heads were nodded in acknowledgement, Ellis' and Purvy's, and one hand was raised slightly, Guy's, but no word was spoken. Bernie mixed the whiskey sour, cursing mentally. You might have known that precious Rex wouldn't have something simple, like a straight whiskey or whiskey and water or a beer. Oh, no. It had to be some fancy damn thing like a whiskey sour that took a lot of time and trouble, and he wasn't fooling old Bernie a damn bit, either. The reason he ordered this kind of crap was because he couldn't stand the taste of whiskey and had to have it doctored up with sweet stuff in order to get it down in his delicate little stomach, that was the reason, and ordinarily it was all right with Bernie, he could drink what he damn well pleased, but it wasn't all right at eight, ten minutes to twelve, and if anyone was thinking he was going to stay even one minute after closing hour, he damn well had another think coming.

Bernie walked around from behind the bar and switched off the lights in the room, leaving only the ones behind the bar itself. He returned and made a few swipes at the bar with his rag and rattled some glasses. He took off his white jacket and put on his street coat. He yawned loudly and scratched his head and looked at his watch.

"Purvy," said Guy suddenly, "why the hell don't you drink your beer?"

"I let it get flat," Purvy said. "I don't intend to drink it."

"Well, for God's sake, why don't you at least quit looking at it like that? You think it's poison or something?"

"No. I was just thinking. I been trying to think who it was."

"Who was?"

"Well, I don't know. I said I didn't, damn it. Down at the depot, I mean. I was watching the seven-o-five come in, and a girl got off and looked around, and then she walked down the platform toward that little park at the south end, and there was someone waiting for her there, and I been wondering who it was. I guess what makes me wonder is why whoever it was didn't just wait on the platform like you'd expect."

There was a period of silence, which was nothing new or different. But it was a different kind of silence. It had a different feel, and even Bernie Huggins felt the difference. It was rather hard to understand, but it was something like the silence in the night when you were a kid in bed, and there was something terrifying off there in the dark that was about to jump and grab you by the throat. It was the silence before your scream.

"You mean it was someone you didn't know?" Guy said finally.

"No." Purvy shook his head. "It was more that I just didn't get a good look at him. He was in the dark down there, and I just got a glimpse of him, hardly more than a shadow, but there was something familiar about him, just the same, the way he moved or something, and it bothers me. You know how a thing gets in your mind and bothers you? I keep trying to think who it could have been."

Guy pushed his double-shot glass away with a kind of violence and stood up. The glass fell over on its side and rolled into the trough along the rear edge of the bar. Bernie picked it up and dropped it into the rinse.

"Well, what the hell difference does it make?" Guy said. "To hell with it. To hell with everything. I'm going home." He was loaded, all right, three shots in the last half hour, plus what he'd had before, but he carried it pretty well, you had to hand it to him, and he walked straight across the room without weaving to the entrance to the lobby. Purvy slipped off his stool and went after him.

"Wait a minute, Guy," he said. "I'll walk a piece with you." Ellis finished his rye and water and spoke to himself, or to whomever wanted to listen.

"That Purvy," he said. "Purvy and his goddamned trains." He got up and walked out, and that left Rex. Rex drank his whiskey sour. At one minute to twelve, he ate the cherry and left also.

*Don't anyone bother to say good-night*, Bernie thought. *Don't any of you snotty bastards bother to say good-night to old Bernie.*

# CHAPTER 7

Purvy caught up with Guy on the sidewalk outside. Turning left on the sidewalk, Guy walked along rapidly with Purvy panting beside him in the effort to keep up. Guy walked with what seemed to be a kind of desperate purposefulness, his shoulders hunched up and his head drawn down inside the upturned collar of his topcoat and his eyes fastened to the sidewalk about two yards in front of his feet.

"Jesus, Guy," Purvy said, "what the hell's the big hurry?" Guy glanced at Purvy with an expression of surprise and impatience, as if he hadn't been aware of Purvy's presence and wasn't very pleased to discover it. He shrugged and slowed his pace.

"Purvy," he said, "what in God's name makes you so damn clumsy? A guy as big as you ought to be able to make a little time without panting like a dog in heat. Don't you ever get any exercise?"

"Well," Purvy said, "the truth is, the men in my family are just bound to be sort of awkward in spite of anything. Take my Old Man, for instance."

"You take him," Guy said. "I don't want him."

"So far as that goes," Purvy said, "I don't want him either, but I'm sure as hell stuck with him."

Guy didn't comment, and the pair of them reached the intersection and crossed it, and Purvy said, "You got your car, Guy?"

"Sure. It's parked down the street at the curb. Why?"

"I thought you might give me a lift home. It's a pretty cold night, what with the wind and all, and it's a hell of a long walk up to the ridge."

"Why don't you get yourself a car, Purvy? Doesn't your Old Man pay you anything for working in the bank?"

"He pays me, all right, but not very damn much. That's not the reason, though. I'm just no good with cars. I get nervous and scared every time I try to drive one. The last time I drove the Old Man's car, I drove it right smack into a tree."

"Hell's fire, Purvy, I thought you always wanted to be an engineer. How the hell did you expect to drive one of those big engines when you can't even drive a car?"

"An engine's different, Guy. You know that as well as I do. It runs on rails, for one thing, and for another, I'd have my heart in it. I wouldn't be scared at all of an engine."

"Well, I'll drive you home, if you want me to, but you'll have to wait a little. I'm going in the Owl Diner down here and have a cup of coffee."

"That's all right. I'll go in there with you. I'm sure as hell in no hurry to get home."

The Owl Diner was a small white stucco building standing next door to a used car lot. Along one side was a short counter with eight stools fastened to the floor at intervals in front of it. It was warm inside, the air fragrant with the scent of coffee and chili and fried onions. With the exception of the proprietor, a thin fellow with a sour expression who was called Cheerful, Guy and Purvy had the place to themselves. They crawled onto stools and sat hunched over the counter, braced on elbows, in the traditional lunch-counter posture. Cheerful, who had been napping in a cane chair behind the counter, roused himself and approached.

"Curly," he said. "Purvy."

"Coffee," Guy said. He rubbed his bad hand across his close-cropped black hair in a sort of reflexive response to the nickname.

"Not for me," Purvy said. "I drink coffee this late, it keeps me awake the rest of the night."

"That's all right, Purvy," Cheerful said. "You don't have to explain why the hell you don't want coffee. Just tell me what you *do* want, that's all."

"Well, I'll have a glass of milk and a piece of butterscotch pie, that's what, and you can go to hell. No wonder they call you Cheerful, you're so damn cranky."

"Sure." Cheerful grinned with sour pride, pleased with Purvy's reaction.

Purvy turned his head toward Guy as Cheerful turned his back to both Guy and Purvy in the execution of his orders.

"What you fellows been doing with yourselves?" Cheerful asked in a tone of voice that made clear his basic indifference.

Guy kept looking into his coffee, which he had not yet touched, and Purvy, prompted by the question, remembered the episode at the station when the seven-o-five came in. He saw again the girl descend to the platform, clearly saw her stand there in her cheap fur coat and look around with that kind of desperate intentness for someone who wasn't there, saw her finally look down the platform toward the south end and move at once in response to a beckoning shadow among the Junipers. That shadow itched Purvy. It itched and itched him, and he couldn't help it.

"I met the seven-o-five," he said to Cheerful. "A strange girl got off, and someone met her. They come in here, by any chance?"

"Here? Why the hell should they come in here?"

"Well, damn it, why not? People get hungry on train rides, don't they? I just thought they might have come in for a bite."

"Seems to me, if she was hungry, she'd have gone in the restaurant at the station. Who was it met her?"

"I don't know. What I mean, I almost know, but not quite. Point is, he was standing in the little park at the end of the platform, and I just barely got a glimpse of him."

"Why the devil would he wait down there in the park?"

"That's a funny thing, isn't it? It doesn't seem like a natural thing to do, does it?"

"Oh, I don't know, come to think of it. It could be natural enough. Maybe it was a guy had a girl coming in to shack up a few days or something. A married guy or someone like that. A guy shacking up sure wouldn't want to parade himself around with the girl on the station platform." Purvy shook his head dubiously, and Guy stood up abruptly. There was in his movement a suggestion of restrained violence.

"You want me to drive you home, Purvy? Come on, if you do."

"You haven't drunk your coffee."

"To hell with the coffee."

He dropped a coin on the counter and went out. Purvy had to wait for the change from a dollar, and when he reached the sidewalk, Guy was getting into his car about twenty yards down the street. Hurrying, Purvy trotted down after him, feeling that his arms and legs were somehow flying in all directions. He wished Guy hadn't made that remark about his being clumsy. Damn it, it was bad enough to be clumsy without having someone always making remarks about it. In the car beside Guy, he sat back and closed his eyes and breathed deeply; When he opened his eyes again, the car was already ascending the tilted street to the ridge where the favored folk of Rutherford lived, which included the president of the Commercial Bank. Looking out across the lawns at the dark houses, he felt sad and impoverished, nagged by a sense of accelerated Time and irreparable loss.

"Time sure goes right along, doesn't it, Guy?" he said, aware that he had made substantially the same remark to Pheeb Keeley earlier in the station restaurant.

Guy shrugged. "It's not Time that goes, Purvy. It's us." Purvy twisted his head around to look at Guy, his eyes popping a little in an expression of surprised delight.

"Say, Guy, that's damn good, you know. How'd you happen to think of that?"

"I didn't. I read it somewhere."

Purvy smiled sheepishly. "I guess I sounded pretty silly about that. You know how those things are, Guy. Something like that just gets in your mind and keeps itching and itching." Guy didn't answer. He pulled into the drive beside Purvy's house, and Purvy got out and said goodnight, and Guy backed into the street again and started down the ridge the way he had come. Passing the Haig house, he slowed his speed and looked up across the deep lawn to the dark windows of the second floor, the corner windows of the room where Lauren slept, and he wondered if she were asleep now, or if she were lying awake in the night, and what, if anything, she wore to bed. It was almost certain that she wore something, for it was somehow impossible to imagine that she did not, and it was also almost certain, at least in his own mind, that she would wear the sheerest of pale gowns over the shadow of her body. Cool, cool Lauren. Cool as moonlight, cool as rain, cool and ever so slightly detached even in response to his advances. Cool and ever so slightly stupid. Cool and more than slightly rich.

Well, he did not object to the coolness of flesh and emotions. He rather preferred it that way, to tell the truth, because it demanded less of him who had given too much too soon to something else. One who quit living to any purpose in his twenties wants in his thirties little more than to live to no purpose comfortably, which entails money, which can, with luck and guts, be acquired by marriage. He could not remember exactly when he had decided to marry Lauren Haig. Neither could he quite remember how he had come to the decision. But however he had come to it, at whatever instant, it was held from inception with abnormal ferocity, and the marriage had become in his mind a kind of desperate alternative to a deadly life of being and having nothing. There were other things he could have done, of course, after the crippling of his hand and the destruction of his precocity. He could have played in minor musical organizations, for which he was more than adequate, or he could have given private lessons, or he could have got a few hours in Education at the University and gone into teaching into some school or other. But it was intolerable to be mediocre in an area where he had excelled, something he could in no way bear. It was better, much better, to be nothing at all—a lousy clerk in an insurance office.

It was not fair, of course, to be forced to such a cruel choice. It was criminally unfair, a monstrous divine crime, but you did not, because of that, overtly cry and whine at God. You merely hated and festered and became cruel in ways that you sometimes regretted. Eventually you merely decided quite coldly to make the best of nothing by marrying a rich girl, a cool and lovely and acceptable rich girl you did not love, and this became established after a while in your mind as more than your privilege. It was your right, your compensation, something God owed you. And nothing would deprive you of it, nothing. Not love. Not conscience. Not God. Certainly no person on earth.

The car descended from the ridge to the level of lower Rutherford, and he began to think of Phyl Bagby and wish that he could go to see her, but this was not possible, or at least not advisable, because of Lauren and of everything that might be lost by imprudence. He regretted Phyl and missed her, far more than she or that clown Purvy Stubbs dreamed or would ever know, and he supposed that he loved her in spite of understanding perfectly well that she had done a lot of sleeping around, which did not really disturb him at all. She had, in fact, a marvelous potential for being a fine friend, as well as a fine lover, and there was in her avid abandonment to pleasure a kind of dry white heat that was clean and consuming and somehow redeeming. She was far removed from Lauren's cool detachment, but on the other hand she was also far removed from the sticky agitation of an Avis Pisano, whom he had taken in the summer in a fetid prelude to disgust and contempt. Yes, he regretted Phyl, her loss, and he missed her, and it was a measure of his commitment to his design on Lauren that he had, without showing the regret or any sign of compunction, excised Phyl from his life.

In a little while, after descending from the ridge, he reached the house in which he still lived with his parents. Leaving the car parked at the curb in the dark street, he went up across the porch and inside.

From the east, over in the railroad yards, came the immense and labored breathing of a slow freight gathering speed.

# CHAPTER 8

Ellis Kuder's car was parked down and across the street from the hotel, about a hundred feet at an angle from the entrance. Ellis crossed to it on the angle and got in and drove west through the Main Street underpass. On the other side of the tracks, after another block of business houses, he turned south and again west into the area of town in which he lived. He felt relieved to be away from his recent companions of the Division Hotel taproom, and this relief, depending on cases, was an effect of different causes. In the case of Purvy Stubbs it was merely the relief of being rid of a clown, a dunce, a clumsy fool and a bore. In the case of the other two, however, Rex and Guy, the cause was something else. He saw Rex and Guy as threats, agents of possible ruin at worst or inconvenience at best, and he began to think now, as he had thought at the bar while being outwardly congenial, that it might become necessary to remove them, and he wondered how, if it came to this, he could accomplish the removal most effectively. That he had known Rex and Guy practically all his life and was ostensibly their friend seemed to have no influence on his thinking. He knew quite well that he was perfectly capable of doing them any dirty or deadly trick that he considered essential to his own ends.

When, he thought, did you first clearly understand yourself, and when, after that, did you finally accept yourself as you really were without rationalization? But this was nonsense, certainly a manifestation of weakness, the idea that there must be between understanding and acceptance a period of squeamish rejection and sickly readjustment. If you were sensible and had any guts at all, understanding and acceptance came simultaneously and without trauma, and you did not create within yourself a futile conflict over what naturally was and could in no way be helped or changed. He did not remember precisely his own first instant of insight, or exactly the incident which prompted it, but probably it was the time he killed the cat. At any rate, though there may have been something earlier, it was the killing of the cat that assumed precedence in his mind. He was a little kid, eight or nine, and he was teasing the cat, a rangy yellow Tom with a temper, and the Tom reached out with a hiss and clawed him. He looked down at the back of his hand, at the thin parallel lines drawn in blood, and there was little or no pain, and the commanding thing suddenly inside him was enormous and icy fury that this filthy beast had the effrontery and the nerve to do this to him, *him*, and there was no retaliation that he was not capable of making. He seized the Tom by the hind legs as he turned scornfully to leave, and he beat the cat's head methodically against the cement walk that ran from the back porch to the garage. When the animal was dead, his proud Tom's head a pulp of blood and matted hair, he, Ellis, carried him back to the alley and lay him on the ash pile and stood looking at him, and all he felt, now that the fury had passed, was a cold and quiet satisfaction and sure conviction that the Tom had damn well got what he deserved. No regret, no compassion, no sense of guilt. Above all, even so early, understanding and acceptance of himself as he was, his potential for deadly retaliation for the slightest affront or threat. Also, deep in his mind, the awareness that this was a menace to himself as well as to others, something which must be controlled and directed for his own security.

Security was, he learned, no more than a matter of developing patience and an alert sense of caution and of being, when the time came, clever enough to avoid exposing himself. Sometimes it was even possible to accomplish what he wished by omission, without taking any overt action whatever, as it had in fact worked out in the case of the boy who had humiliated him and later drowned. At this time he was in high school, a junior, eight years after the killing of the imprudent Tom, and there was this girl whose name no longer mattered that he wanted for himself, as his steady girl, for as long as it might please him to want her. He was proud, as he had the right to be proud, and it didn't occur to him that the girl would reject him on his own terms, not really, and when she did foolishly reject him, it was a shameful thing that could not pass, and what made it even worse was that he was rejected in favor of the other boy, the one who later drowned. It was very foolish of this boy to be preferred. It was just too goddamned bad.

He, Ellis, could not handle this as he had handled the Tom, by means of sudden and satisfying reprisal, and so he waited and waited and lived patiently with his shame and the unsettled score that survived his interest in the girl, which had not lasted long anyhow, and eventually reprisal was secured quite adequately by accident and by omission. A group of them was on this wiener roast at the small lake seven miles north of Rutherford, and it was dark, and everyone was across the lake in the picnic area except him and this boy, and since it was late and after dark, the pair of them decided to swim across, rather than walk around the end, which would save time. They started out together, and it was quite a long way to swim, and about three quarters of the way across, something happened to the boy. A cramp or something. The boy called for help, but he, Ellis, simply swam away and left him, and so he was even at last without any investment in danger to himself, and no one ever knew or guessed what was done or not done or for what reason. He went on to the picnic area in the low region beyond the dam and reported that the boy had drowned in spite of his efforts to reach him and save him, and he watched the girl who had started it all go into the ugly antics of hysteria, and he wondered why in God's name he had ever thought he wanted her in the first place. Other than that, his only feeling was one of requital.

There was never, in short, any particular pleasure in ruthlessness for its own sake. The pleasure was in the awareness of the grand potential to accomplish without remorse or excessive emotion whatever might be required by condition. As in the war. As in the instance, which was only one among many, when he climbed the slope to the ridge from which the enemy had recently withdrawn under fire. The dead were around him, the scattered remnants of men, and among the dead remnants were three living, the deserted wounded. They lay together at the base of a tree, their breathing labored and harsh with suffering and terror, and one of them opened his eyes and looked up with irises fevered and supplicating in enormous whites. He stood holding his BAR in his hands and considered objectively what should be done about the three wounded men, and it was obviously a convenience and a precaution against possible treachery from behind to kill them, and so he raised the BAR, and the wounded man who was looking at him closed his eyes, and he shot the three of them as methodically as he had once killed the Tom, but this time there was no rage, and on the other hand neither was there any particular excitement or regret or aftermath of depression.

He was, in fact, scornful of excessive demonstration of any kind in the business of killing and trying to escape being killed in which he and the other men in his outfit were engaged. With those who showed a kind of adolescent savagery in the moratorium on the sixth commandment, keeping score as if they were playing in some kind of new and exciting and bloody game, he despised equally those who were shaken and disturbed and brooded on their guilt. As for him, he killed in necessity without compunction, and he was not fool enough to waste time afterward in either exultation or regret. In the meanwhile, in accordance with his early understanding, he took all possible precautions to avoid putting some individual among the enemy in the position of exulting or brooding over Ellis Kuder.

Now, over a decade later, in a dark street in the southwest part of Rutherford, he stopped his car in front of a large old house with a porch running completely across the front and half way to the rear on one side.

The house was constructed of clapboard, elaborately decorated with gingerbread. Once it had been the private residence of a prosperous merchant who had built it before prosperity's general trend to the ridge to the east, but the merchant was now dead, his family dispersed, and the house was the property of a real estate dealer who rented it out as two small apartments on the lower floor and four sleeping rooms above. Ellis had one of the rooms. Although his father was dead, his mother still lived in her own home in town, but he preferred not to live with her. He had discovered immediately after the war that living with her was scarcely tolerable any longer, and so he had moved away, and he had remained away in spite of entreaties to return. His mother was a dull woman, full of platitudes and engaged in good works. He hardly ever saw her.

Upstairs in his room, he dropped his topcoat and suit coat onto a chair and went into a small private bathroom, which was something the other second floor rooms did not have, and for which he paid a small premium. After turning on the light above the lavatory, he removed his shirt and washed his face and hands and brushed his teeth. In the cloudy mirror on the door of the medicine cabinet, he examined briefly the good lines of his face, the shining curly hair that was so dark a red that it seemed at times actually to be black with red highlights. His reflection gave him a feeling of satisfaction that was, besides being a tiny part of his total enormous vanity, a simple recognition of the value of appearance as a tool. Turning away from the mirror, he returned to the bedroom, leaving the door partly open behind him to permit the entrance of a swath of light that cut diagonally across the floor below the foot of the bed. Outside the swath, in the shadows beyond it, he stripped to his shorts and lay down on the bed. It was warm in the room, much too warm for sleeping, and it would be necessary after a while to get up and cut off the radiator and open a window, but now he did not want to sleep, could not have slept had he wanted to. Lying quietly on his back and looking up at the bathroom light striking diagonally across the dark ceiling, he began to think of Lauren Haig and to wish that she were beside him on the bed in the dreary rented room. His desire for Lauren was strong and genuine and would have existed even if she had been poor instead of rich. He did not feel love, for there was no tenderness in his feeling, which was something he felt for no one and was incapable of feeling for anyone, but it had endured for a long time and would continue to endure.

It was only Lauren who now kept him in Rutherford, which was, God knew, a miserable hole of a town. He had returned to it after the war only because he was familiar with it and had thought that he could manipulate it easily to his own advantage, especially as a war hero, but he had been unable to do it and had grown sick to his belly of it long ago, the ugliness and frustration and enervating dullness of it, and he would have gone away for good if it had not been for Lauren, whom he desired, and Lauren's wealth, which he also desired. His desire for both antedated only slightly the calculated determination to possess them, Lauren and what Lauren had, the beginning fully four years ago of a careful scheme of conquest which now, he felt, was approaching a successful end if only some goddamned emotional cripple like Guy Butler or some mother-smothered ass like Rex Tye did not in some way cut him out and louse things up for keeps. Or if he did not louse it up himself by damn fool carelessness such as he had been guilty of, for instance, in the sordid little gonadal episode with that panting bitch at Sylvan Green last summer. Thinking of Avis, he felt sick, and thinking of Guy and Rex, he felt a rising cold resentment that approached the quality of fury. Though he did not consciously think so, he reacted to their encroachment as if it were deliberate insolence, a kind of intolerable violation of his person, as the Tom's had been, as later the boy's had been in the matter of the girl who was, in herself, not very significant.

But Lauren was significant. In herself and in what she stood for, she was vastly the most significant individual on earth, excepting Ellis Kuder only, and her significance was based on both his genuine desire and his realization that he could never in the world by the exploitation of his own assets, even shored by his almost perfect ruthlessness, escape from the terrible mediocrity that was in him and around him and was slowly smothering him from within and without. A million or so dollars, or the prospect of them, did not alter mediocrity, but they made it possible to live with it compatibly. They made it possible to bear the whole vast encroachment and corruption of a life otherwise unbearable.

He lay on his bed in his rented room, and Lauren lay beside him. He reached out in the darkness and touched her body, her cool taut flesh, and he felt in her flesh the quivering of passion against restraint, the agony and excitement of capitulation.

After a while he got up and went into the bathroom and turned off the light and came back into the dark bedroom. He cut off the radiator and opened a window and lay down again, now under the covers. Lauren was no longer in the bed with him. He was completely alone. He heard in the railroad yards the same laboring freight that Guy Butler heard.

# CHAPTER 9

Rex Tye closed the front door of the house carefully. There was only the faintest click when the latch slipped into place behind him. A small table lamp, left burning by his mother, spread its weak light thinly on wall and floor, and the shadows beyond the perimeter of light seemed to press upon it and wait and wait with infinite patience for the time when they could close in. Quietly, for several full minutes without moving, Rex stood by the door with one hand still on the knob. He listened to the house, the whispers of the house, the stirring and breathing of wood and fabric and the immaterial residue of things said and done and felt. A tiny night-light was burning in the wall at the head of the stairs, and he lifted his eyes to it and looked at it steadily for quite a while, and he thought that the light on the table in the hall and the light in the wall at the head of the stairs were somehow symbolic of his mother, of his mother and him and their relationship, and everywhere he had ever gone, or went now, or would ever go, he would find little trails of weak light that she had left in the darkness to show him the way.

There would be a light in his room, too. The last thing she had done before going to bed, he knew as certainly as if he had witnessed it, was to go into his room and light the lamp which was now there burning for him, the last of the three to show him the way. She had left the light and gone to bed, but she had not gone to sleep, and she was lying and waiting for his return now in the darkness of her room upstairs, and he believed that there was no sound in the night too soft for her to hear, not even the rush of air into the place his body vacated in movement, and quite possibly she had already heard the tiny snick of the latch which even he, right next it, had hardly been able to hear.

He wondered why he hated his mother so utterly. It was easy to understand why a clown like Purvy Stubbs hated his Old Man, for one was a coward and the other was a bully, and so hatred was natural between them, but it was by no means so easy to understand why he, Rex, hated his mother, and there were many obscure forces involved in it. Not that he really wanted to understand it, or tried seriously to analyze it. It was so enormous and virulent inside him that it justified itself in its simple enormity, and far more astonishing that its existence was the incredibly natural cunning with which he had all his life concealed it. He had always been a courteous and considerate child, and he was a courteous and considerate man, and he performed the superficial functions of devotion with a kind of consummate ease, so that they could, though it was not suspected, be as naturally the expression of animus as otherwise. In a minute, for example, he would go upstairs and open his mother's door and speak to her, and she would be awake and would respond, and he would go in and sit on the edge of her bed, as he always did, and they would talk for a while, and he would kiss her good-night, as she would never in the world suspect that he wished she were dead for no other reason than that it was the only way she would ever leave him, while it was somehow impossible for him to leave her. And this was something else he could not understand: that he could not desert her, though he wished each time they parted never to see her again.

Moving abruptly with a suggestion of effort, as if against a compulsion to remain indefinitely where he was, he walked over to the hall table and turned off the lamp and went upstairs. In the upper hall, he stopped at the head of the stairs and looked at the floor outside his mother's door, which he had to pass in order to reach his own, and there was no sign of a light yet, but he knew that she was awake and waiting and perhaps even at that instant reaching for a switch, and as he watched and anticipated it, the light appeared in a thin bright line at the door's bottom edge. Promptly, responding to an invitation that had the authority of a command, he went to the door and knocked and entered.

His mother was sitting up in bed with her pillow bunched behind her back. Her gray hair had been undone and brushed and brought over her shoulders in two parts, but it was not otherwise disarranged and had obviously not touched the pillow that supported her back, and it was clear that she had been sitting erect in the darkness awaiting the sound of his return. There were blue shadows in the gray hair, and blue shadows under the eyes that looked at him levelly across the room with an expression of adoration that was a kind of refined and subtle wickedness. It possessed, he thought, the ugly narcissism of a cultist who had created his own esoteric deity in his own image.

"Hello, Mother," he said, closing the door of the room behind him.

"Hello, darling." She patted the bed beside her with a thin, blue-veined hand. "I was hoping you'd stop to chat with me. I've been quite unable to sleep."

He walked over and sat on the bed in the precise place the hand had indicated. He held the hand in one of his and began stroking it softly with the other. It was somehow essential to their relationship to sustain the fiction that this was all charmingly casual and unplanned, with nothing demanded or conceded, although he always stopped, and she never slept, and everything was done and said almost with the practiced precision of a ritual.

"Have you had a pleasant evening?" she said.

"All right," he said. "Nothing exceptional."

"Perhaps you would like to tell me about it. I'm always so interested in hearing about your affairs, you know."

He hesitated before answering, and there was, after the hesitation, a thin edge to his voice.

"It's hardly worth telling, Mother. The evening was really quite dull."

This was a deviation from the ritual, and he felt her hand stiffen in his. The hand was very cold, he thought. Why was her flesh always so cold when she kept her room so warm?

"I'm sure I'd not find it dull," she said, "but it is unnecessary to tell me about it, of course, if you don't wish. How is Lauren?"

"Lauren? Lauren's fine."

She was silent again, clearly waiting for him to tell her whether or not he had seen Lauren tonight, but he looked down at her hand, tracing with his eyes its blue veins, and volunteered nothing. She was not certain, but she thought she detected in him a hint of deliberate recalcitrance, and it disturbed her and made her a little angry, and she was forced to prolong the silence until she was quite sure that the anger would not be apparent in her voice.

"She's a sweet girl," she said. "Quite unspoiled, in spite of her family's wealth. I was very pleased when you and she became such close friends, darling."

"I know, Mother. You want me to marry her, and I am more than willing, in spite of her family's wealth."

Irony was something he had never used against her, and it was cruel and terrifying in its implications of what might develop between them, or might be secretly between them at this moment, and she felt suddenly tired and venomous and exceedingly old. But she ignored his remark, waiting again for the assurance of control, for it was imperative that nothing he brought into the light that might grow there. In the dark, things withered and decayed and did not grow.

"You look tired," she said. "Would you like to go to bed?"

"I think I would, if you don't mind. It's rather late, really. I stopped in at the taproom of the Division Hotel at the last minute."

"Do you think the taproom is really a proper place to go?"

"There's nothing wrong with the taproom, Mother. I met Guy Butler and Ellis Kuder and Purvy Stubbs there tonight."

"Really? That's nice. They're all quite acceptable friends, I'm sure."

*Oh, Jesus, Jesus, Jesus*, he thought. *Because Guy was precocious and almost famous, and because Ellis Kuder's mother is a dull woman involved in good works, and because Purvy's Old Man is president of a bank and lives on the ridge, it follows with some kind of odd logic that they must necessarily be acceptable to anyone, and it does not matter or refute the logic in the least that Guy is a psychic cripple and near-alcoholic, or that Ellis is capable of committing any atrocity that suits his purpose without jeopardizing his security, or that Purvy is a frustrated incompetent, festering with hate and guilty of mental patricide at least. It is quite acceptable to associate, even in a taproom, with these honorable young men of Rutherford, even though I am, of course, superior to all of them, in spite of their superior advantages, and this is something taught to me by my mother that I believe. I believe in my own superiority as something that does not have to be demonstrated or proved, the result of a sort of laying on of hands or spiritual visitation, and whether the hands and spirit were of God or the devil is also something that does not matter in the logic of my mother.*

Leaning forward, he brushed his mother's forehead with his lips. The perfunctory kiss was like a touch of dry ice, and he caught from her thin blue nylon bed jacket a faint scent of nauseous lavender. Abruptly, he stood up.

"Good-night, Mother. I hope you will be able to sleep now."

"I don't feel that I shall. I'm sure I shall lie awake all the rest of the night."

"Have you taken anything?"

"No. I don't want to develop a dependence on soporifics. They become a habit, I understand."

"I doubt that one tablet would do you any harm. Would you like me to bring it to you?"

"Do you mind? The box is in the medicine cabinet in the bathroom."

He went into the bathroom and found the box, a shiny green cardboard container with a pharmacist's label pasted on the top. Closing the cabinet door, he caught a glimpse of his reflected face below shimmering pale curls. It was a face that gave the impression of delicacy without actually being delicate in the structure of bone or the molding of flesh. His mother had told him once that he looked like pictures of Percy Bysshe Shelley, and he had thought himself, after finding a picture of Shelley in an anthology, that there was a resemblance. His mother had told him also that she regretted not having thought of Shelley as a Christian name for him, which was a regret he shared. It seemed to him much more appropriate than Rex, his father's name, and when he was quite young he called himself Shelley secretly and sometimes in school wrote it over and over in his notebook.

After filling a water tumbler about a quarter full from the tap of the lavatory, he carried the tumbler and the barbiturate into the bedroom. Handing the tablet to his mother, he stood watching while she swallowed it, and then he handed her the tumbler and waited again until she had drunk the water, which she did quite slowly in small sips. Taking the tumbler from her hand when it was empty, he set it on her bedside table.

"Are you ready to lie down now, Mother?"

"Yes. I think so. Perhaps I shall sleep after all."

"If you'll just lean forward a little, I'll arrange your pillow."

"Thank you, darling. You're very considerate."

She leaned forward as he suggested, and he arranged the pillow in its proper place, and smoothed it with his hands and helped her to lie down with her head upon it.

"Good-night, Mother," he said again. "Shall I put out the light?"

"Yes, please."

He turned out the light and bent over from the waist in the exaggerated immediate darkness to kiss her a second time, the dry ice touch and scent of lavender, and then, without speaking, he went out of her room and down the hall to his own. He undressed at once and put on his pajamas and sat down in a chair beside his bed and stared across the room at the wall, and for a while he saw nothing whatever, because his eyes were blinded by the thoughts behind them, but then he became aware of a large photograph of a man and a woman and a child. The photograph was hanging on the wall, where it had hung for as long as he could remember, and the man was his father, the woman his mother, the child himself. He had been about seven, he thought, when the picture was made, and his father had died during the winter following, and it was a long time ago. He did not remember his father very well, and he would not have been able to recall the father's appearance at all if it had not been for the picture. He had learned, however, from things said and suggested and perceived dimly in the shadows of old conflicts in his mother's mind, that his father had been a timid, introverted man, a material failure, the worst possible kind of man to have been married to the woman he was married to, a woman of velveteen arrogance and fierce ambition. He had learned from his mother to despise his father, the memory of him. Most of all, he had learned that he was somehow dedicated to compensating the mother for the father's inadequacy. He had not so far, however, been or done anything exceptional at all, and he had, like his father, been deprived in his turn of his proper position. There seemed always to be a kind of conspiracy against him, the right combination of qualities and circumstances never quite falling out together, and it was not fair, it was simply not fair.

But now the conspiracy had collapsed. Now he saw that he would actually achieve the position that had been withheld, and it was as simple as a seduction, although a polite and proper and subtle seduction. He would marry Lauren Haig. This was an objective to which he had for a long time been dedicated, except for the single insane lapse last summer at Sylvan Green, and the vanity which was essential to his survival did not for an instant permit him to doubt that he would in the end be chosen over Guy Butler or Ellis Kuder or anyone else who wished to compete. For he was Rex Tye. On him had been laid the hand.

Thinking of Guy and Ellis, he smiled thinly. He knew perfectly well that they didn't like him, though they treated him with courtesy and accepted him with reservations. This did not disturb him, however. On the contrary, it rather pleased him. They disliked him because of his air of fastidious superiority, and their very recognition of it gave it validity.

He heard the freight that Guy heard, that Ellis heard, and he went to bed.

# CHAPTER 10

The one who murdered Avis Pisano fell asleep and slept for almost two hours and awoke suddenly for no particular reason that he could isolate and identify.

*Murderer*, he thought. *Murderer*.

The thought was like a whisper coming from a dark corner of the room into the darker cavity of his skull. It moved like the merest breath of air in the deep night over the contour of his brain.

*Murderer, murderer, murderer.*

He was not afraid of the darkness or of what the darkness held, for that fear springs from a sense of distinction, of being apart and alien and vulnerable, and he and the darkness were one. He lay on his bed and listened to the slow and cadenced breathing of the night, which was also his own breathing, and the pulse of the night was in his throat and was measuring time behind his eyes. In his mind, with a precise and exceptional clarity, he began to recall the chronology of the night, and he was standing again in the little park among the Junipers, and it was cold, and the Junipers rustled in the wind. The cold penetrated his clothing and his flesh and crept into his bones. He cursed the cold and beat his hands, and from far down the parallel shining rails came the thin and distant cry of the seven-o-five. The cold now diminished by an intense and rising sense of hot excitement, he watched Avis Pisano descend from the train and peer about her in the yellow light, and he stepped forward among the rustling Junipers and raised an arm, and then there was instantly a dissolution and reassembling of time and action, and he was walking slowly over the frozen ground of the shallow slough with her dead weight in his arms, and her hair hung down and swayed with his walking as if it possessed a separate and continuing life of its own.

Bending his knees with the right foot forward of the left, he descended into a kneeling position, as one might kneel to receive an accolade, and then bending the trunk of his body forward from the hips, he laid the body he carried upon its back on the frozen ground, and afterward arose and brought his left foot up even with his right and stood for a moment looking down with bowed head in a posture of prayer or mourning. Above him, the moon slipped silently into an unclouded space, and the light of the moon touched the eyes of Avis, and she stared upward into the light with wide-open eyes through a lacery of black branches to the moon itself. In spite of her facial distortion and visible tongue, she acquired in that moment of light an ethereal quality she had never had, a brief and capricious delicacy in death.

Turning away, he walked back up the dry slough to the road, and there was another dissolution and reassembling, and he was back in an instant at the railroad station, in the windswept park among the Junipers, and there was a fat fool standing in the yellow light on the platform beside the restaurant door, and the fool was a deadly menace.

Purvy. Purvy Stubbs. That odd obstructed clown to whom striped overalls and a striped cloth cap were as much a fetish as the cloak of Christ. Recapitulated now, leaning like a bloated adult child against the station in the windy cold, he possessed a gross and obscene quality that was like the innocent evil of an idiot. He was not a joke, as he had always been, no longer despicable and fit for contempt, for he had become by chance, or perhaps design, a potential agent of ruin. How much had he seen? Well, very little. That was apparent from his comments in the taproom at the Division Hotel tonight. But how much significance was attached to the little? That was the threat and the essence of terror. Perhaps it would be, then understood, a clear clue to identity. If so, how long would it be before Purvy's tumbling brain recovered the clue and achieved understanding?

Fear probed the sheltering darkness and touched him and made him cold. He had felt no remorse, and felt none now, and would feel none ever, and what he had felt primarily, almost to the exclusion of other emotions, was an enormous exhilaration and pride that he had accomplished decisively so monstrous much. Avis Pisano had been a cheap little fool with the temerity to threaten him, and she had received nothing that she had not deserved and made necessary by stupidity, but now he was threatened again by another fool, and what made it worse, what made it utterly infuriating, was that the threat this time was not the conscious action of a directed intelligence, however inadequate, but the intolerable meddling of an inferior who had been placed by accident in a position to destroy him. Anger came, the cold fury with the cold fear, and he tightened the muscles of his body and lay rigidly looking up into the darkness, but he could not control the trembling which had seized him, and this was degrading and humiliating and took the fine edge off his sense of pride and power.

Suddenly he got up and stood beside the bed, and the icy air from the open window cut at his flesh and was like a blow above the diaphragm. In a gesture of defiance, as if it were imperative now to show his contempt for everything that threatened him or tried to hurt him, he walked directly to the window and stood there looking down at an angle to the street until he was numb, and then it occurred to him that his display of defiance was in itself a form of weakness, a concession to amorphous beings, and so he closed the window and returned to the bed and sat down on the edge of it.

*Lauren*, he thought. *Lauren*.

Thinking of her, forming in his mind the shape and sound of her name, he tried also to see her as she might be at that instant, and for a moment he succeeded. Lying in a softer, warmer darkness, she slept and breathed, and her breath stirred sweetly on her lips. Her breasts, with the breathing, rose and fell, and her white legs moved in sleep to a need she would not remember.

She receded, returned and was changed.

She lay on her back and stared blindly at the moon.

She was gross and obscene in a too-short coat in a wash of yellow light.

The murderer pounded a fist into a palm and cursed the gross image.

He lay down under covers and closed his eyes, but he could not sleep, and the night in time became day.

# CHAPTER 11

Purvy Stubbs was an early riser. There were two reasons for this, neither of them indicating on Purvy's part any particular addiction to industry or the homely wisdom of Poor Richard. In the first place, by rising early and breakfasting at once, he was able to avoid the company of his Old Man at table, which was more than compensation for the loss of a little sleep. In the second place, he liked to go down to the station and watch the eight-ten come in from the south, and it was necessary to allow sufficient time for dressing and eating and the walk to town. For the first two hours of the day, as a matter of fact, he functioned on a schedule that was almost as precise as that of the trains. He set his alarm for six-thirty, rolled out immediately, shaved and dressed and was downstairs at seven, allow a minute or two either way. He took a full half-hour for breakfast, being a hearty eater, and he always had three scrambled eggs, six slices of crisp bacon, three cups of coffee with sugar and cream, and biscuits with jam, or toast with jam, depending upon which was served to him by Verbenia, the Negro cook, who loved him far more than anyone else on earth.

The second morning after the murder of Avis Pisano, which was the morning of Monday, he entered the dining room at two minutes before seven. His breakfast was ready and piping hot, a pleasure to see, as well as to smell and taste, white and yellow and shades of brown, and he wondered if anyone had ever written a poem about scrambled eggs and bacon, but he couldn't think of any. Then he tried to think if something of the sort had been written in prose by Thomas Wolfe, who had written quite a lot about food in general, but he couldn't remember anything like that either. He ate his breakfast slowly, left the house at seven-thirty, and reached the station at seven-fifty-five.

The wind had died in the night, but it was still pretty cold. Purvy went through the waiting room onto the platform and directly down to the restaurant. To his surprise, Phoebe Keeley was still inside the oval counter. She looked tired and cross.

"Hello, Pheeb," he said. "What the hell you doing here this hour? I thought you worked six to six."

"That's what I thought, too," Phoebe said. "The truth is, Madge Roney is working six to six days, or's supposed to be, but she called in and said she couldn't make it till eight and would I stay on. What can you do when someone calls and asks will you stay on?"

"Well, I guess you have to stay, when you come to think of it. Tough luck, Pheeb."

"Oh, it comes out all right. Madge'll stay on till eight tonight, so it all comes out all right."

"Still, twelve hours is a hell of a long shift, especially at night, and fourteen's just too damn long to expect. I bet you get pretty tired, Pheeb. Along about three, four in the morning, it must get pretty tough."

"It's not so bad, to tell the truth. Matter of fact, six to six nights is a hell of a lot better than six to six days, in my opinion. Days are busier, and your feet catch it. You're always on your feet without even any chance to sit down more'n a minute or two at a time, and your feet ache and all. Nights, especially after midnight, it gets pretty quiet usually, just a few customers now and then, and you can sit around quite a bit without being disturbed, and I've even been known to catch forty winks, but don't tell the boss. I got seniority over Madge and could have the day shift if I wanted it, but the simple truth is, I won't have it."

"I can see your point of view, at that, come to think of it. There sure are advantages to the night shift, Pheeb, there's no question about it."

"Of course it ties you down a lot. Concerning dates and things like that, I mean. You only get one night off a week for dates and all."

"That's right. There are advantages and disadvantages, sure enough. I guess that's the way it is with everything."

"I guess so. You want a cup of coffee, Purvy?"

"No, thanks. I had three cups at home. Fact is, I'm floating."

"Well, why didn't you stop in the men's room? You came through the station, didn't you?"

"I came through, all right, but it hadn't struck me yet. You know how these things are. Pheeb. It just now struck me."

"You better go on back while you got time."

"Oh, it's not that bad yet. I can hold it until the eight-ten comes in."

Phoebe leaned on one elbow on the counter and looked at Purvy, who had seated himself on a stool, with an expression of affectionate tolerance. She shook her head slowly from side to side.

"Purvy," she said, "you're the goddamndest fellow I know anything about, if you don't mind my saying so. I'd give a good tumble to know what it is you see in these lousy trains."

"I've tried to tell you, Pheeb, but I can't seem to get across."

"That's right. That's damn sure right, Purvy. I'm ready to say that I'll simply never understand it. I guess it would take one of these psychologists or someone like that to see what's really behind it."

"Well, it's sort of interesting. Pheeb. You'll have to admit that."

"The hell I will! What's interesting about a train?"

"Oh, the people coming and leaving, going places and all that. You wonder where and why, I mean. It's interesting to wonder. You take Saturday night, for instance. A girl got off the seven-o-five, Pheeb."

"Really? Now, that's really interesting, Purvy. That's about as fascinating a piece of news as I've ever heard. A genuine live girl with two legs and everything?"

"You needn't be so sarcastic, Pheeb. She got off, and she was wearing this fur coat, and looked around like she was expecting someone, and then she saw this person down in the little park at the south end of the platform, and she went down there and disappeared."

"In the park? That little patch of grass with the Junipers growing in it? Why would anyone wait down there?"

"Well, that's what's interesting about it. It looks to me like whoever it was would have waited out on the platform."

"You mean you didn't see who it was?"

"No. Just a sort of shadow. I was telling Cheerful Forbes about it Saturday night, and he said it was probably someone who had this girl coming in to shack up or something."

"That sounds reasonable. Whose wife is gone? You know anyone?"

"No, I don't, Pheeb. I haven't heard of anyone. It could have been someone from another town close by, as far as that goes. It would be smart to have her get off at another town than the one you lived in."

"Purvy, I do believe you'd be real good at having some sneaky affair with someone. It sounds to me, as a matter of fact, like you've got it all figured out how to do it."

"Oh, come off, Pheeb. You just get to wondering and figuring, and things like that come into your head, that's all."

"Well, you ever decide to lead a life of sin, you let me know, Purvy. I might be interested."

"You oughtn't talk like that, Pheeb. Someone who didn't know you might think you were serious."

Purvy looked at his wrist watch, more to avoid Phoebe's eyes than to read the time. Then he stood up suddenly and walked over to the big plate-glass window.

"Say, Pheeb," he said, "the eight-ten's late. It's eleven after already."

"Lord God!" Phoebe said. "The world's coming to an end!" At that moment, as if to refute her, the whistle of the eight-ten drifted up faintly from the bend of the tracks to the south, and Purvy, since it was so cold outside, stayed standing by the window to watch it arrive and depart. While this was being accomplished, Madge Roney arrived and took over in the oval, and when Purvy finally turned away from the window, the train gone, Phoebe was standing beside him with her coat on.

"Purvy," she said, "you got a car here?"

"No, I haven't, Pheeb," he said. "I don't drive. Didn't you know that?"

"You don't drive? Why the hell not?"

"I just don't have the knack for it."

"Damn it, Purvy, anyone can drive if he tries."

"I can't. I've tried and tried, but I keep running into things."

"Oh, well, never mind. It's just that I'm pretty tired after fourteen hours, and I thought you might drive me home."

"I'd sure be glad to, Pheeb, if I had a car and could drive it. If you want me to, I'll walk home with you, though."

"What the hell good would that do? Purvy, you do come up with the damnedest things sometimes. I'll just go in the station and call a taxi."

"Okay, Pheeb. I guess I'd better be getting on down to the bank, myself."

"So-long, Purvy. See you when the trains come in."

"Sure, Pheeb. So-long."

She went out onto the platform and walked north toward the waiting room doors, and Purvy stood and watched her through the glass. He liked Pheeb a lot, even though she ribbed him and sometimes got sarcastic. The nice movement of her big hips was pretty much concealed by her coat right now, but it didn't make any difference to Purvy one way or another. He went out into the cold himself and started for the bank and got there about twenty-five after eight, which was twenty-five later than he was due, and thirty-five before the doors opened.

Purvy worked as a teller, but he wasn't very good at it. He made far more mistakes than a teller was ordinarily allowed. Every once in a while his Old Man, when he was particularly aggravated by something Purvy had done, would come out of his office and say in a loud voice for everyone to hear that he was damn well tired of tolerating endless stupidity and was damn well having Purvy's hands measured for a broom handle. This had disturbed Purvy at first and had caused him to feel humiliated and ashamed, but the Old Man killed the effect by over-doing it, the same way he killed all his effects, and after a while Purvy didn't pay much attention to it, and neither did anyone else. It was all bluff and bluster, anyhow. The Old Man wouldn't really have put Purvy to sweeping the floor and polishing the brass on the front door, which work was now done by a fellow named Wendell who had eaten some lye as a baby and had his mind affected by it, for it would have been a reflection on the Old Man himself to have Purvy doing such menial work around the bank. He just bluffed and blustered and threatened, and all the other employees were secretly on Purvy's side.

The morning went by pretty pleasantly, once the doors opened and it got started, and the one thing about being a teller that Purvy liked was the opportunity it gave him to exchange little bits of talk with all the different people who came in to deposit money or take it out or to see about having Purvy's last mistake corrected. Between eleven and noon there was quite a rush, which was usual, for it was then that the business places up and down Main sent someone in to do their banking for the day, and at noon, when things slacked off, Purvy went to lunch. He didn't go home, because his Old Man would be there. Most of the time he went to the coffee shop at the Division Hotel, and that's where he went this particular day. He didn't go directly into the coffee shop, however, but into the lobby, where he stopped at the desk to exchange a few words with Chick Jones, the day clerk.

"Hello, Chick," he said. "Let me have a package of those Kools and a package of Black Jack chewing gum."

"Jesus, Purvy," Chick said. "Menthol and licorice! You sure got peculiar tastes."

"Oh, I don't know. You get used to mentholated cigarettes, you don't want anything else. At least, that's the way I find it. As for the Black Jack, I been chewing it ever since I was a kid. When I was a kid, I thought a stick of Black Jack was about the best treat there was, and I guess I've just never gotten over it. Matter of fact, my Old Man says I've never gotten over most of the things I liked when I was a kid. How are things going, Chick?"

"Okay, Purvy. Everything quiet."

"No wild parties in the rooms, or anything like that?"

"Nope. Maybe a little quiet fornication, but no wild parties."

Chick laughed, and so did Purvy. Purvy opened his pack of Kools and offered it to Chick, who declined. Purvy lit one himself and puffed up a little cloud of mentholated smoke. He never inhaled. He just drew the smoke into his mouth and blew it out through pursed lips, just exactly as he had smoked dried grape vine and catalpa beans years ago. It was something else he had never gotten over.

"You happen to remember the guests who checked in Saturday night?" he said.

"Not exactly. Man and his wife, I remember. Half a dozen salesmen."

"Oh. No strange girl?"

"Nope. No girl at all, strange or otherwise. Why, Purvy? You fixing up one of these assignations or something?"

He laughed again, clearly considering this too ludicrous to be taken seriously.

"Nothing like that, Chick," Purvy said. "You know damn well I don't have anything like that to do with women. The truth is, I'm just curious. I saw this girl in a fur coat get off the seven-o-five down at the station Saturday night, and I'm just wondering who she is and where she went and all. You know. Just curious about it."

"Well, she didn't check in here, and if she got sneaked up without registering, someone owes the balance on a double, that's all I can say. I don't give a damn who sleeps with who, but they can't do it for the price of a single."

"All right. Chick. I was just asking out of curiosity, that's all. Guess I'd better go in and get some lunch now. See you later."

"Sure, Purvy. Take it easy."

Purvy went into the coffee shop and had sweetbreads for lunch, and afterward, about twenty to one, he came back into the lobby and looked into the taproom and saw Guy Butler sitting on a stool at the bar. The taproom opened at twelve-thirty, and Guy was probably the first customer. He would probably, at midnight, be the last. Looking at him, Purvy remembered the bit from Housman about malt doing more than Milton can to justify God's ways to man. Guy didn't drink beer, of course, only bourbon, but the principal was the same. Purvy went in and sat beside him at the bar.

"Hi, Guy," he said.

Guy didn't look at him. He swallowed some bourbon and said hello. Bernie Huggins came up opposite, and Purvy said he guessed he'd have a short beer.

"What you mean, guess?" Bernie said. "You want a short beer or not?"

"Goddamn it, Bernie," Purvy said, "gimme a short beer."

Bernie drew it and shoved it across the counter. Purvy picked up the glass and looked at it. He didn't really want the beer, but he felt that he had to order something to justify his presence. As a matter of fact, he didn't even know exactly why he was present. He didn't have anything in particular to say to Guy, but somehow he always felt impelled to be friendly whenever he saw Guy around, even though Guy couldn't always be said to be responsive.

"How are things going, Guy?" he said. "You're starting early, aren't you?"

"This is breakfast," Guy said.

Purvy understood that this was Guy's way of telling him to mind his own damn business, but Purvy didn't resent it because he deserved it, and it seemed that he was always saying something innocently that had the sound of meddling.

"I asked Chick Jones if that girl who got off the train checked in Saturday night," he said, "but Chick says she didn't."

Guy turned his head then and looked at him for the first time. He looked at him levelly without any expression whatever for thirty seconds at least, and he didn't say a word. Then he turned away and took another swallow of bourbon and looked into his glass, still not saying a word, and Purvy realized that he had done it again, given the impression of meddling when he didn't really mean it that way at all. He gulped his short beer, wiped his mouth, and slid off the stool.

"Well," he said, "I got to get back to the bank. Be seeing you, Guy."

"Chances are," Guy said.

Purvy went back to the bank and got into his cage, and the afternoon drifted along uneventfully and was generally pretty dull until ten minutes to three, the closing hour, when Mrs. Brisket came in to deposit her pension.

"Hello, Mrs. Brisket," Purvy said.

"Hello, Purvy," Mrs. Briskett said. "I've simply never heard of anything so terrible."

"What?"

"I say it's simply terrible, isn't it?"

Purvy remembered to look to make sure that Mrs. Brisket had endorsed her check, which was something she usually forgot to do and he forgot to check, but since he had remembered this time, so had she, of course, and he thought that she sounded like she was thoroughly enjoying the most terrible thing she had ever heard of.

"What's terrible, Mrs. Brisket?"

"You mean you haven't heard?"

"I guess not. At least I haven't heard anything that struck me as being particularly terrible."

"That young woman being murdered, I mean. Hadn't you heard?"

"No, I hadn't. I hadn't heard."

Purvy made a neat entry in Mrs. Brisket's little black account book. His hand was steady, and he felt quite calm, and it crossed his mind that this was something he had a right to be proud of.

"Someone found her in a slough southwest of town," Mrs. Brisket said. "Her body, that is. It was a farmer, I think, who found her. Or maybe someone hunting rabbits. Anyhow, whoever found her, she had been strangled to death and left there in the cold for heaven knows how long, poor thing, and Sheriff Lonnie Womber went out and brought her into town to Haley's Funeral Parlor, and she's lying there this instant."

"Who is this young woman?"

"No one seems to know, Purvy. Anyhow, as I heard it, no one has been able to identify her yet. Seems she was a perfect stranger around Rutherford."

"Did you hear how she was dressed?"

"Dressed?"

"I mean her coat. Did you hear what kind of coat she was wearing?"

"Oh, yes. Now that you ask, I did. It was fur. Some kind of fur."

"Thanks, Mrs. Brisket. Do you need any blank checks today?"

"I don't think so, Purvy. I'm sure I have plenty, thank you very much."

Purvy pushed her account book through the aperture, and turned and walked right out of the cage and out of the bank without even bothering to put on his hat or topcoat. Haley's Funeral Parlor was on Main Street, a couple of blocks beyond the edge of the business district, and he walked directly there and went inside into the little hall outside the chapel, and Lonnie Womber was standing there talking to Mr. Haley.

"Hello, Purvy," Lonnie said. "If you came to see the girl, you can't."

"If she's the one I think she is," said Purvy, "I could tell you something about her."

Lonnie looked at Purvy for a few seconds. He had a long face with a long droopy nose and squinty eyes. His hair was the color of straw and straight as string and hung over his forehead almost into one eye. He looked shrewd, and folks said he was shrewd, and probably he was. For a county sheriff, anyhow.

"In that case," he said, "you better look and see if she's the one."

"It's all right," said Mr. Haley. "We haven't started to work on her yet."

They went into one of the back rooms, and the body was lying on a long table under a sheet. Lonnie pulled the sheet back a little, and Purvy looked at the distorted face of Avis Pisano.

"It's her, all right," he said.

He had thought she looked cold and lonely on the station platform night before last, and now he thought she looked colder and lonelier than ever. He felt all of a sudden like crying.

# CHAPTER 12

The county jail was a yellow stone building sitting on a corner among a grove of walnut trees. In the fall, when the walnuts dropped, the kids in the neighborhood came and gathered them and took them home to spread out for drying. The juice in the hulls stained like dye and had to wear off, and for a long time afterward you could tell the kids who had gathered walnuts by the brown stain slowly fading to yellow on their fingers.

Inside, in Lonnie Womber's office, the air smelled of strong soap and men's bodies and sweeping compound. Overhead, suspended from the ceiling at a point determined by drawing diagonals from opposite corners, was one of those old-fashioned fans that beat the air slowly in the summer and made a kind of sleepy, satisfying sound that is not quite comparable to any other sound in the world. The fan was now still and had acquired a cobweb between its blades. Looking out a high, narrow window from his position in a chair in front of Lonnie's desk, Purvy could see a brown branch of ivy extending from the vine that climbed the yellow stones out of view to the right. The branch of ivy shivered in the wind and sometimes scratched at the glass.

"All right, Purvy," Lonnie said. "Now tell me what you know about this girl who was killed."

He was sitting behind his desk in a swivel chair. He rocked back in the chair and lifted his feet onto an open drawer of the desk. He acted as if this were all just pleasant conversation that didn't mean anything in particular one way or another.

"Well," Purvy said, "the only thing I know, as a matter of fact, is that she got off the seven-o-five Saturday night, and someone met her."

"Is that so?"

Lonnie found a cigarette paper in a vest pocket and a can of Prince Albert in his coat pocket. He shook a little tobacco into the paper and rolled it up and ran his tongue along the gummed edge of the paper. Some people said it was an affectation for Lonnie to smoke roll-your-owns instead of tailor-mades, that he did it because it made him seem more in the character of an old-school sheriff, and others said maybe not, maybe he simply preferred them, and the truth was, he smoked them because they were cheaper. He lit this one with a paper match and let it hang from the corner of his mouth. Smoke ascended from it in a very thin blue line.

"Well," he said, "it might not seem like much at first thought, but when you stop to consider it, it's quite a lot. We can find out where the train came from, the towns it stopped and all, and we ought to be able to find out where the girl got on it. Chances are we can find someone to identify her without too much trouble. Who was it met her? That's the important thing right now, as I see it."

"I don't know."

"You mean it was a stranger?"

"No. I didn't actually see whoever it was, that's what I mean."

"Then how the hell you know *anyone* met her?"

"Damn it, I mean I just got a glimpse of whoever it was. He was waiting down in the little park with the Junipers in it. It's dark down there at night, and I just saw a kind of shadow or movement or something, and the girl saw it, too, and went down there. That's the last I saw of her until a while ago in Haley's."

"You used the third person masculine singular." Lonnie looked rather proud of this bit of erudition which might not have been expected from a county sheriff. "How do you know it was a he?"

Purvy looked surprised, not so much as a result of Lonnie's knowledge of pronouns as of the question itself. Now that he was forced to think of it, he didn't know why he assumed that it was a man who had waited in the cold and windy darkness among the Junipers, but he just knew damn well it was, that was all. Still, there must have been a reason. A reason, that was, for the assumption. Something seen, something almost registered, something slipping in an instant into the shadows. His brain began to itch again, and it was simply the most aggravating feeling in the world to be unable to scratch it.

"I don't know, Lonnie," he said. "I don't know how I know, but I'm damn sure, just the same, that it was a man."

"Well, considering developments, it's likely that it was, at that. Did this girl have a bag or anything when she got off the train?"

"Yes. One bag. She picked it up and carried it with her when she went down the platform to the little park."

"All right. We haven't been able to find it, so someone took it away. Whoever killed her, no doubt. Buried or burned by now, probably. We may find a trace of it later, but I doubt it like hell." Lonnie removed the roll-your-own cigarette from his mouth and looked at it sourly. It had gone out, so he threw it into a number 10 can on the floor and stood up. "Confidentially, Purvy, I never had a murder on my hands before, except the one couple years ago when that crazy half-breed killed the farmer over his hay-pitching wages, which was all cut and dried, with witnesses and everything, and damned if I know just what to do to get started. I guess I ought to try to get this girl identified, first off. What do you think?"

"That's what seems logical to me," Purvy said. "Seems to me you can't do much of anything at all until you know who she was."

"The seven-o-five's a local, isn't it?"

"That's right."

"Well, that's a break, at least. It ought to be easy to check back on the passengers in a dinky little local. Maybe the conductor would remember something. I guess the railroad could tell me who the conductor was, and where he lives. If he can remember where the girl got on, we got a big jump on things. I really got no confidence in its turning out so nice and easy, though. I got a feeling the conductor won't remember a damn thing about anything."

"Even if he doesn't, you could check the towns on the line. There can't be so very many on a short run like that."

"That's true. You got a good head on your shoulders, Purvy."

"Another thing. If the girl's got a family or something, they'll probably report her missing after a while. If they don't hear from her or anything, I mean."

"Sure. If she's got a family. If she was the kind who kept in touch with her family, if she had one. If her family's the kind that would worry if she didn't. If to hell and back."

"Well, damn it, you can publish a picture and description and all, can't you?"

"Purvy, damned if you don't make me completely ashamed of myself. By God, maybe you ought to be sheriff instead of me, and I ought to go down to the station and watch the trains come in and go out. Well, I guess we can't arrange a shift like that, though, because the people elected me to this office, and I got to do the best I can, and that's all there is to it."

While talking, Lonnie had come around the desk and put an arm around Purvy's shoulders, and all of a sudden, without quite understanding how it had been accomplished, Purvy found himself at the office door and being guided through into the hall. He felt proud that he had been able to contribute something valuable to Lonnie in the matter of the murdered girl, but he didn't swallow Lonnie's bull about his own inadequacy, not by a long shot, and he knew perfectly well that Lonnie had already thought of all the things that he, Purvy, had mentioned—like being able to check the towns, and publishing a picture and description and all—long before Purvy had thought of them himself. It was part of Lonnie's character to belittle himself, except at election time, and a lot of smart guys around the county had taken it at face value and gotten careless and were a hell of a lot sorrier and wiser afterward.

"Well, I haven't done much, really," Purvy said. "I just happened to see the girl get off the train, that's all."

"I'm damn glad you did." Lonnie gave Purvy's shoulder a pat that was also enough of a shove to get Purvy all the way through the door into the hall. "You've been a big help, and I appreciate it. Good-bye, now."

He closed the door, and Purvy went down the hall and outside and started back to town, and he kept thinking about the dead girl and feeling terrible about her, worse and worse as he walked, and he decided he would go to the taproom at the Division and have a drink and see if there wasn't someone around to talk with. It helped make things a little lighter inside you if you could talk about them with someone. He wondered how it would be, watching the seven-o-five come in after this. He was certain his pleasure in it would be spoiled a little, at least for a while, and this was added to his sorrow for the girl and made him feel even more terrible than before.

It was a few minutes after five when he reached the hotel and went into the taproom, and the bar was doing a modest business. Guy Butler was there, on the same stool, in the same position, over a different glass. From appearances, he seemed not to have moved since noon, but this was not so. He had gone through the routine of his job, at least, and had just returned to the taproom. Next to him sat Ellis Kuder, and down the line, two Pabst Blue Ribbons intervening, Rex Tye sipped a whisky sour and seemed, between sips, to be inordinately preoccupied with the cherry. Purvy claimed an empty stool somewhat removed from all three. He climbed on and specified a shot of bourbon when Bernie Huggins got around to him. Bernie, who had been reaching for a short beer glass, looked at Purvy in amazement, his body posed in a position of arrested motion.

"Purvy," he said, "if I didn't know damn well better, I'd swear you said you wanted a shot of bourbon."

"That's what I said," Purvy replied, "and you know it."

"Okay, okay. It just requires a little adjustment, that's all." Bernie set out a glass and poured from a bottle. "What's the matter, Purvy, you had a bad experience or something?"

"As a matter of fact, I have. I been down to Haley's Funeral Parlor looking at that girl who was murdered." Conversation died down the bar. A focal point and feeling suddenly uneasy about it, Purvy gulped his shot, gagged, took a quick swallow of water. Then he felt more assured, a little important. Bernie Huggins leaned across the bar and peered closely into Purvy's eyes to see if he was telling a whopper. Purvy plainly wasn't.

"The hell you say!" Convinced of Purvy's sincerity, Bernie straightened and continued to stare across the bar with a great deal more interest than Purvy ordinarily elicited. "How come you been doing that? You acting as Lonnie Womber's deputy or something, Purvy?"

"You know I'm not any deputy, Bernie. It just happened that I knew something that turned out to be helpful."

"Is that a fact? Can you tell us about it, or is it a secret among you sleuths who are working on the case?"

This was meant to draw a laugh along the bar, but everyone was concentrating on Purvy and missed the humor. As a matter of fact, the only one who got it at all was Purvy himself, who didn't appreciate it. He flushed and looked at all the faces turned in his direction. All but two, that was. Ellis Kuder looked straight across the bar into the mirror at his own reflection. Guy Butler looked into his glass as if he hadn't the slightest awareness of what was going on around him. Rex Tye stared steadily at Purvy down the length of the bar, but his face was no more than a white blur in the dim light that did not touch it directly.

"You needn't try to be funny about it, Bernie," Purvy said, "because it's a long way from a joke. The way it happened, I was at the station Saturday night when the seven-o-five came in, and this girl got off. She was all alone, and I had a feeling, when Mrs. Brisket told me in the bank about a girl being murdered, that they might be the same. It was just a kind of feeling, I mean. I went down to Haley's to see, and they were, and that's all there is to it."

"Did you know her, Purvy?"

"No, I never saw her before. Before Saturday, that is. The first time I ever saw her was when she got off the train alone and stood there looking around like she was expecting someone who had forgotten to come. I felt sorry for her for some reason or other, and that's a fact, and I guess that's the reason I looked at her close enough to be able to recognize her a little while ago at Haley's."

"Where did she go, Purvy? Which way from the station, I mean. Did you notice?"

"Well, she walked south down the platform, but I don't know which way from there. There was someone waiting for her, and they must have gone away together."

"I thought you said she looked around like she was expecting someone who had forgotten to come."

"That was before she saw him, and that's the queer part of it, seems to me. Someone was waiting for her, all right, but he was down there in the dark in that little park where the Junipers grow, and he never did come out into the light. I just got a glimpse of him. Just a kind of movement, if you know what I mean."

"You mean someone was actually waiting for her? She went off with someone?"

"That's right. That's what I mean."

Purvy looked at his empty glass and wished it were full, and Bernie, as if reading his mind, immediately fulfilled the wish. Bernie seemed hardly conscious of what he was doing, and all along the bar there was no sound or movement from any of the early drinkers as the full significance of Purvy's words became apparent. Into the warm taproom crept the cold of the little park, and it was suddenly as if the murderer sat among them.

Which, of course, he did. He sat in the cold and said nothing and listened to the whispering Junipers.

"Jesus," Bernie said. "Jesus."

# CHAPTER 13

The man standing beside Lonnie Womber in the back room of Haley's Funeral Parlor plainly wished that he were elsewhere, but he was as plainly resigned to the doing of his duty. He stood looking down at his pot belly like some sort of odd philosopher seeking peace in the contemplation of his navel. Across the belly, threaded through a button hole of the vest and stretching on either side to opposite pockets, was a massive silver chain. Automatically, although he was not now on schedule and had no particular place to be at a certain time, the man removed from one of the pockets the heavy watch that was attached to one end of the chain. This was a gesture of habit, and he did not even read the time. Replacing the watch, he resumed the contemplation of his belly and did not look up immediately when Lonnie coughed and nudged him gently with an elbow. It was apparent that it required some effort to do what was required of him, and he was not to be hustled into doing something he would have preferred not doing at all.

"All right, Mr. Craddock," Lonnie said. "If you'll just have a good look at her and tell me what you think."

Mr. Craddock lifted his eyes then to the exposed face of Avis Pisano, and after the initial shock, it wasn't quite so bad as he had anticipated, and there was even a kind of quietude in the face, a suggestion of release that was less disturbing than the drawn look of illness that it had worn on the train. He stared at the face for almost a full minute without stirring, and he thought that there was really no sign that the girl had died violently, murdered, except the marks on her throat. This surprised him a great deal. He hardly knew what he had expected to see, but certainly something. Some ineradicable mark of evil and terror to indicate the enormity of this death.

"Yes," he said. "Yes."

"Yes, what, Mr. Craddock?"

"This girl was on the train, all right. I remember her particularly because she looked ill, and I felt sorry for her, and asked her if I could be of any help, but she said no. I remember that she kept looking out the window with this blind look in her eyes that people get sometimes. Not seeing anything. Just looking. I thought she was ill."

"Probably she was."

"Sort of nauseated and feverish, that is. As if she might be taking flu or something."

"She was pregnant."

"Pregnant? You say she was pregnant?"

Mr. Craddock looked slowly around at Lonnie, and then reluctantly back at the face of Avis, dreadfully certain now that the indicative mark of monstrous evil would surely be there, and he was surprised again to see that it was not. Only the suggestion of quietude and release.

"That's right, Mr. Craddock," Lonnie said. "Post-mortem showed it up."

The thought of the post-mortem was extremely unpleasant to Mr. Craddock, although he was uncertain as to what exactly was done in one, and he had for one moment the terrible feeling that he was going to humiliate himself by being sick to his stomach. He turned abruptly, standing with his back to the body, and assumed the same briskness of tone that he might have used with the porter on his train.

"What do you want me to tell you, Sheriff? I hope that I won't be detained much longer."

"After a couple of questions you are free to go, Mr. Craddock. To begin, now that you have been good enough to verify that she was on the train, I'd like to know the name of the town where she boarded it. It will be a big help if you can remember it."

"There's no problem there. I collected her ticket just this side of Twin Springs. Therefore, since tickets are collected between each stop, that's where she boarded."

"Twin Springs, then. Thanks very much, Mr. Craddock. Twin Springs isn't a very big place, and it ought to be easy enough to get some information about her there. Tell me. Were you on the platform when she got off? Here in Rutherford, I mean."

"Yes. I was standing by the steps when she came down from the coach."

"Did anyone meet her?"

"I don't think so. I don't remember seeing anyone on the platform except that fellow who always hangs around. He was standing over by the restaurant door."

"Purvy. Purvy Stubbs. He meets nearly all the trains. He's a nut about it. Well, thanks again, Mr. Craddock. You've helped me out a lot, and I won't keep you any longer."

"You're welcome, I'm sure."

Mr. Craddock took two steps toward a door that opened onto the rear drive where he'd left his car, and then he stopped, stood motionless for a moment, and turned very slowly, as if under a compulsion he tried to resist, to look back a final time.

"I'm sorry," he said, "I'm truly sorry," and it was impossible to tell if he was speaking to Lonnie or to the body of Avis.

Under way again, he walked briskly to the door and out into the drive, and although Lonnie followed him immediately, he was in his car, the car in motion, before Lonnie arrived. Standing under a permanent awning that extended over the drive outside the door, Lonnie watched the car turn into the street and disappear, and he wondered if he had better drive to Twin Springs today, or if it could be postponed until tomorrow, and he decided reluctantly that it could not be postponed and that he would have to go.

First, however, he returned to his office in the county jail. From a drawer of his desk, he took a brown manila envelope that contained three photographs of Avis Pisano, all from different negatives and all taken in the back room at Haley's. Standing by the desk, he looked at the photographs one at a time slowly, the varied perspectives of the serene death mask. He felt a little sick, a little angry, but most of all he felt afraid, and what he feared was not what he knew, but what he might learn. After a few minutes, slipping the photographs back into the manila envelope and the envelope into the right side pocket of his coat, he went out and got into his Ford and drove through town on the Main Street to its intersection with a north-south highway. Turning north, he drove steadily for two hours, about a hundred miles, when he stopped at a highway restaurant for a cup of coffee. The coffee was inferior, and he smoked two cigarettes with it. This required altogether about fifteen minutes, after which he returned to the Ford and drove for slightly longer than two more hours and slightly farther than another hundred miles. It was just before two o'clock in the afternoon when he reached Twin Springs.

He was hungry by that time, eight hours removed from breakfast, and he was tempted to eat before doing anything else, but he resisted the temptation and drove first to the railroad station. The depot was wooden, painted an ugly mustard yellow, separated from the tracks by a narrow brick platform. He parked in a graveled area at one end of the platform and crossed the bricks to the entrance. Inside, in the small waiting room, along three walls, there were the kind of hard oak benches that are apparently designed for the purpose of making people prefer to stand. In the center of the room was a pot-bellied cast-iron stove with a scuttle of coal on the floor beside it. In the fourth wall, from left to right as it was faced, were a door marked Ladies, the agent's grill, a door marked Men. Lonnie went to the grill and peered into the room beyond. There was no one there, and so he waited patiently, leaning against the grill beside the aperture and utilizing the time to roll and light another cigarette. After a while, a door opened, admitting to the agent's office a gust of cold air and a small man who seemed to be propelled by it. The man took off a wool mackinaw and a wool cap that matched it, hanging the mackinaw on a hook in the wall and stuffing the cap into one of its pockets. Then, rubbing his hands, he approached the grill and peered through at Lonnie, who turned to face him squarely. The agent was wearing bifocals which had steamed over when he came inside, and he took them off, wiped the lenses on a blue bandana handkerchief, replaced them on his nose. He held his chin tucked in against his chest so that he could look easily above the insets in the lenses.

"What can I do for you?" he said.

Lonnie introduced himself and took the manila envelope out of his coat pocket. Removing the photographs, he pushed them through the aperture in the grill.

"You know this girl?" he said.

The agent studied the pictures carefully, holding them in a stack neatly and slipping the top one off and putting it on the bottom as he went through them. He looked at each picture a second time before he pushed them back to Lonnie through the aperture.

"She looks dead," he said.

"That's because she is."

"Why you interested in a dead girl?"

"She was murdered. Last Saturday night. In Rutherford or near it."

"Oh. That one. Remember hearing it on radio, now that you mention it. Didn't actually hear it myself, to tell the truth. My wife heard it and told me about it. Hardly ever listen to radio myself. You the sheriff, you say?"

"That's right."

The agent shook his head. "I don't know her."

"You sure?"

"Never seen her before. Not to my recollection."

"Maybe your recollection isn't so good. She came to Rutherford in the local the day she was murdered. Saturday. She boarded it here. Could someone else have sold her the ticket?"

"Nope. If she bought a ticket here Saturday, I sold it to her."

"But you don't remember? It was only three days ago."

"Can't help that. I still don't remember her. Maybe I sold her the ticket, and if what you say's true, I guess I did, but I got no recollection of it just the same."

"You'd probably remember her if she were familiar to you, wouldn't you?"

"Probably."

"I thought maybe she lived here in Twin Springs."

"Maybe she did. I don't know everyone who lives here, son.

"It isn't a very big town."

"Neither's Rutherford. You know everyone there?"

"Okay. I get your point. But tell me this. You remember selling a ticket on the local to *anyone* Saturday?"

"Seems I did. Two or three, it seems. But I couldn't say who. In the first place, I never pay much attention. Second place, I don't see so well. You're a little blurred yourself, son."

"You think you'll remember me three days from now?"

"Don't be sarcastic with me, son. If she lived here in town, you ought to find someone who knew her."

"Sure. No offense. Thanks for trying."

Carrying the envelope with the photographs in it, Lonnie went outside and got into the Ford. He started the engine so the heater would operate and sat thinking. He supposed he ought to contact the chief of police, as a courtesy if not for information, but first, he decided, he would go get something to eat. Having made the decision, he turned in the graveled area and drove up the main street of the town until he came to a short-order lunch room. Parking the Ford in front, he went inside and ordered two hamburger sandwiches with apple pie and coffee. The hamburger was greasy, the apple pie was too dry, but the coffee, unlike that in the highway place, was aromatic and hot and very good. He drank it and was grateful for it and ordered another cup. He was the only customer in the place at the time. The waiter, who was probably also the owner, was a beefy fellow with a heavy red face beginning to hang on its bones. He leaned against the back counter with his arms folded across his chest, a toothpick hanging from his mouth. Every once in a while, he made a soft sucking sound, and the toothpick was briefly agitated. The name of the lunch room, established by the identification painted on the front window, was Ed's Place, and it was therefore likely that the name of the man was Ed. This was also soon established.

"You the owner?" Lonnie said.

"That's right."

"Lived in Twin Springs long?"

"All my life."

"Business good?"

"Lousy. Lousy business, lousy town."

Looking into his coffee cup and sniffing the rich aroma, Lonnie had an idea. Not much of one, really. Just something that might, with good luck, pay off. The idea was that girls are sometimes waitresses, and Avis

Pisano, for no particular reason that he could justify, had seemed to be the kind who might have been.

"You ever hire a waitress?" he asked.

"Sure. Got one now. Mornings and evenings. Afternoons are slow. After one-thirty or so. I handle afternoons myself."

Lonnie took the manila envelope out of his pocket, removed the pictures, spread the pictures on the counter facing Ed.

"You ever seen this girl?" he said.

Ed leaned forward from the hips, his backside maintaining contact with the back counter. He was very still, giving an effect of sudden rigidity, staring intently.

"It's Avis. Avis Pisano." He looked up abruptly, his eyes wary. "Who the hell are you?"

*Avis*, Lonnie thought. *Avis Pisano.*

So that was her name. That was the peculiar arrangement of symbols and sounds that had given her identity, and still did, and the sounding of it now gave her also an added substance, a reality she had somehow not quite possessed previously. For the first time since he had gone out to the dry slough and looked at her staring blindly at the sky through the black branches of trees, she was in his mind a person who had lived as well as died, who had been called something, by a name, had written it on school papers, at the end of letters, on the fly-leaves of books, in and on the thousands of perishable places where one identifies oneself for an instant of infinity.

Now, in response to Ed's question, he established again his own identity in his own instant. He told the beefy proprietor who he was, and what, and how Avis had died.

"Did you know her well?" he said.

"Pretty well. She worked here a couple of months last winter. Early this year, it was. January, February, maybe part of March. With spring coming, she quit and went out to Sylvan Green to work. It's a resort out on the lake, and she could make more money there, what with tips and all."

"Did she live here in town?"

"She did. Had a room at Mrs. Gorman's. Old place over on Sage Street, about three blocks from here. After the season was over at Sylvan Green, she came back there, I understand, but she didn't ask for her job with me back. I had another waitress, anyhow."

"When did she come back from this Sylvan Green?"

"End of September. Sometime around then. The hotel there is open year-round, but it doesn't do a hell of a lot of business in the winter."

"Does she have a family in town? Any relatives at all?"

"No family anywhere that I know of. Her folks used to live on a farm out west a piece, but they're dead. Avis had moved into town even before they died, when she was about fifteen, at a guess. She worked around, here and there, waitress jobs and the like." He hesitated, looking down at the spread of photographs as if he were reluctant to say what was in his mind. "She developed a kind of reputation," he said.

"Reputation?"

"Round heels."

"Oh." Lonnie gathered his pictures and returned them to the envelope. "I guess I better go see this Mrs. Gorman. Where did you say she lives?"

"On Sage. Three blocks north, straight over. It's a big house with gingerbread. Needs paint. You can't miss it."

"Thanks," Lonnie said.

He went out to the Ford and drove north and found the house that needed paint in a block of houses that needed it. He crossed a rickety porch and rang a bell and waited. Pretty soon the door was opened by a woman with a massive torso, sagging at breasts and belly, that seemed to be balanced precariously on thin, bird-like legs.

"Are you Mrs. Gorman?" he asked, removing his hat and allowing his hair to fall immediately over his forehead, almost into his eyes.

"Yes," she said. "What do you want?"

"Does an Avis Pisano have a room here?"

"She does, but she's not in."

"Where did she go?"

"Out of town. She left last Saturday, and I don't know when she'll be back."

"I know when. Never. She's dead."

"What?" The woman's mouth fell open, exposing unbridged gaps between remnants of teeth. "What happened to her? How did she die?"

Again Lonnie identified himself, offering proof. He explained everything he thought the woman ought to know, which was, at this point, practically everything he knew himself. Her flaccid face, as he talked, assumed a variety of expressions, including brief concessions to horror and compassion, and settled at last into the lines of a final judgment that encompassed neither.

"I can't say it's entirely unexpected," she said. "I always felt she might come to a bad end."

"Is that so? Why?"

"She was not a good girl. She permitted men to go to her room."

"Really? Did you permit her to have them there?"

"I disapproved, and said so, but she was past her majority and paid her rent. It was not my place to dictate her behavior."

"I see. Well, I don't mind saying that I admire a person with a tolerant attitude. May I see her room, please?"

"If you consider it necessary."

"It might be helpful. You never can tell about such things." He went into a dark hall and past an iron radiator that hissed at him. Following Mrs. Gorman upstairs, he had a closer look at the bird-like legs and wondered again how they functioned and survived. In an upper hall a few feet from the head of the stairs, he was admitted to the room in which Avis Pisano had lived, had washed and dressed and dreamed and slept and made love, and there was nothing there, no scrap of a thing, that made him feel that she had done any of those things, or had really ever been there at all. He went through her possessions in closet, in drawers, wherever they were found, and nothing spoke to him, nothing answered what he asked. Eventually he left and went back downstairs and said good-bye to Mrs. Gorman in the lower hall. Outside on the porch, he decided that it would be a futile gesture to see the chief of police. He would, instead, drive immediately to Sylvan Green, which he could reach, he thought, around dark.

He was accurate in his estimate, reaching the hotel minutes ahead of darkness. The water of the lake at the foot of the slope was still as glass, a sheet of burnished gray that glittered darkly in the fading light. The litter of cabins among the black trees along the shore were dark and obviously unoccupied. The rustic hotel, affecting unpeeled logs and heavy timbers, showed light at three upstairs windows and at the windows of the lobby below. The light from the lobby windows spilled out across a high, wide porch of thick planks. Mounting steps, Lonnie counted them. There were an even dozen. Crossing the porch, he entered the lobby.

When the spring and summer vacation season was over, guests were few at Sylvan Green. Hunters came now and then, alone or in small groups, to stay a few days and tramp the low hills covered with leafless scrub oaks, and there was a nominal amount of overnight patronage by transients who preferred the accommodations to those of inferior hotels in the towns of the area, but it barely paid to keep open after September, and affairs were managed by a skeleton staff. In the lobby now, a man in a wool plaid shirt was talking by the tobacco counter to a man in a red flannel shirt, and another man in a gray business suit was reading a city paper in an upholstered chair with maple arms and legs. Besides these and Lonnie, only the clerk was present. A blond young man of effeminate mannerisms, the clerk leaned on the counter with languid limpness and watched Lonnie approach with an expression that seemed to suggest that he would rather Lonnie didn't.

"I'd like to see the manager, please," Lonnie said.

Somewhat to his surprise, the languid blond claimed that distinction for himself, and once again, with increasing weariness in the routine, Lonnie explained who and what he was, the purpose of his visit. This time, for which he was grateful, there was no necessity to show his collection of pictures. That bit of his approach made him feel illogically surreptitious, as if he were somehow soliciting attention to obscenity. Besides, the clerk-manager was sufficiently shaken by the unadorned report of murder, and Lonnie did not wish to add the shock of the dead face.

"Avis Pisano was employed here last summer, I believe," he said.

"That's right. As a waitress."

"I wonder if I may see your register for that period. Say the months of July and August."

"Certainly. Would you care to step into the office?"

"I would, thanks."

Going around the counter, Lonnie crossed the small space behind and passed through a doorway into an office that was no larger. There was a desk and a chair, of which he assumed the use, and the clerk-manager placed in front of him a file box of registration slips approximately five by eight inches in size. Alone, the other having excused himself and returned to his desk, Lonnie went through the slips slowly, reading the meaningless signatures, and in the end there was still no meaning, and he was vastly relieved. Rocking back in his chair, he rolled a cigarette and lit it. Squinting through the thin blue smoke, he thought of something that destroyed in an instant his abortive relief, and after a few minutes he stood up reluctantly and crossed to the door and spoke to the blond.

"Do you have a separate file for the cabins?" he asked.

The manager said that they did. He came back into the office and got it. Again alone, Lonnie started through it, turning each slip with a feeling of dread that seemed to acquire more intensity in each instance, and when he was finished at last, the dread had been justified, and he sat back and closed his eyes and pressed against the lids until he was compelled to relax the pressure by unendurable pain. He felt sick, violated by a kind of odd anger that was partially inverted for no good reason, and he wished that he were not a sheriff and in no way involved in what he was. It had been, moreover, a long, long day, and he was suddenly bone-tired. It would be possible, of course, to take a room in the hotel for the night, but he had a desire to get away that was stronger even than the attraction of a bed, and the desire was actually a compulsion to be moving at once toward a necessary end. Getting up abruptly, he went out into the lobby. The manager and the three guests watched him in a hiatus of silence, and he understood that he had been reported and discussed. There was no justification for his resenting this, but he did, and he thought tiredly that he would have to guard his emotions. It wouldn't do at all to become excessively irascible just because he had a rotten job that he'd asked for.

"I'm finished now," he said to the manager. "Thanks for your help."

He crossed the lobby, followed by four pairs of eyes. Outside, he stood for a minute on the porch, listening to the night. The lake was so still that it made no sound. In the Ford, he began the long drive back to Rutherford.

# CHAPTER 14

Purvy Stubbs didn't think very fast, and he knew it. He also knew that he talked too much. He had even learned from experience that slow thinking and excessive talking are an unfortunate combination that can often get a fellow into trouble, a condition to which Purvy was no stranger. It was no wonder, then, that it took him quite a while to understand that he might now be in danger because he was himself a danger to someone else. To a murderer. It was not pleasant, when you finally came to consider it properly, to be the only person on earth to have seen a particular murderer in damning circumstances. Of course, Purvy had not actually seen the murderer, not to recognize him, but he had got a glimpse of him, a shadow among shadows, and what was worse he had opened his big mouth frequently since to say that there had been something vaguely familiar about the shadow that itched his mind, something significant that he was trying to isolate and pin down.

Suppose the murderer was in town. Suppose he had even sat quietly in his personal hell and listened to Purvy talk like this. Purvy did suppose, finally, and he felt cold and miserable. He wasn't ashamed to admit that he was afraid, in fact, and when the fear really got powerfully into him was the afternoon that Lonnie Womber had him down to the office in the county jail for a talk, which was the afternoon of the day after Lonnie went to Sylvan Green. What made the fear somehow more terrible than it would otherwise have been was that it was inspired by someone, not precisely known, who was probably quite familiar and had never inspired fear before. It was like when you were a kid in the dark, and the friendly objects of your room betrayed your mist and became enemies, and even the room became a trap.

It was after two in the afternoon when Lonnie called Purvy on the telephone, and things were slow in the bank.

"That you, Purvy?" Lonnie said.

"Yes," Purvy said.

"Lonnie Womber here. You busy?"

"Not very. You know how it is in the bank in the afternoon, Lonnie. Things are slow."

"I was wondering if you could come down to the jail for a little talk."

"Well, damn it, Lonnie, I'm supposed to stay on the job whether we're busy or not. The Old Man doesn't like me to be running off before quitting time."

"This is pretty important, Purvy. I don't think your Old Man would object under the circumstances."

"What you want to talk with me about?"

"Telephone's no place, Purvy. I'll tell you when I see you."

"Is it about what I saw at the station?"

"Look, Purvy. Just get the hell down here to the jail, will you, please?"

Purvy could see then that Lonnie was determined that he was going to come, and so he said he would and hung up. After all, Lonnie was a sheriff, which is a kind of cop, and he probably had the authority to order you around if you were involved in something, and he might even be able to make trouble for you if you didn't do as you were told. The Old Man was in his office with his door closed, talking to a farmer about a mortgage or something, so Purvy didn't bother to report that he was leaving. As a matter of fact, he hadn't spoken to his Old Man about the girl at the station, and how he had got himself involved by just being around at the time, and if he had his way in the matter, he wasn't ever going to say anything about it, for his Old Man would sure as hell cuss him out and call him all kinds of a bumbling fool who couldn't manage to stay out of trouble even when he was standing around doing nothing. He got his hat and put on his too-short topcoat and walked across town to the jail.

Lonnie was in his chair with his feet on the half-open drawer. The door to his office was open, and Purvy stopped at the threshold, waiting for an invitation to cross. Lonnie looked at him sourly, looked away at the dead cigarette in his fingers. The cigarette was coming apart at the seam, and Lonnie threw it into the number 10 can on the floor with more force than was necessary, a display of restrained violence against something unidentified for which the cigarette was a symbol. He didn't bother to stand, or even to lower his feet.

"Come on in, Purvy," he said. "Better shut the door." Purvy did both. He sat in the chair beside Lonnie's desk, holding his hat in his lap. Lonnie's expression, still sour, seemed to imply that Purvy was something of a trial, to say the least, which was an attitude on Lonnie's part that Purvy could in no way understand, since he had been helpful and had put Lonnie on the track of something.

"Purvy," Lonnie said, "has it occurred to you by any chance that you sometimes talk too much?"

Since it had, Purvy was forced to admit it.

"As a matter of fact, it has," he said, "and if you mean about seeing someone in the little park at the station, it's been on my mind and worrying me."

"That's good, Purvy. You just keep on worrying. If you recognize something and worry about it enough, chances are you keep ready to take care of it, if necessary."

Lonnie took time at that point to start the construction of another roll-you-own, and it was Purvy's opinion, not expressed, that if Lonnie wanted him to worry, he had sure as hell made a good start toward accomplishing what he wanted.

"You trying to scare me or something, Lonnie?" he said. Lonnie didn't answer immediately, and when he did answer, not directly. He finished his cigarette and lit it and looked at it for a moment as if it were offensive.

"I took a little trip yesterday, Purvy," he said. "Up to Twin Springs."

"Twin Springs? Why'd you go to Twin Springs?"

"Because that's where this girl who was murdered got on the train. I learned that from the conductor, who happened to remember her, and I went up here to find out who she was. Her name was Avis Pisano."

"Avis Pisano," Purvy said.

After saying the name aloud, he repeated it three times silently, fashioning the shapes of the sounds with his lips so carefully that Lonnie was able to read them clearly. And to Purvy, as it had to Lonnie, the name gave substance to the one who had used it, making her real and her death a real death, the sad bad end to which she had come in Rutherford.

"Last summer she worked as a waitress at Sylvan Green," Lonnie said. "I went out there, too. I checked all the registrations for July and August."

"Why for then? I mean, why just pick out July and August?"

"Because it was about that time, somewhere along there, that Avis Pisano became pregnant."

"Pregnant? Who said she was pregnant?"

"The doc says it. Haven't you ever heard of a post-mortem, Purvy?"

Purvy had heard of it, all right, but he didn't want to think about it now. The truth was, he was wishing desperately that he hadn't been on the station platform that night. It was the first time in his life that he actually regretted having seen a train come in and go out.

"You think she was murdered because of that?" he said.

"I think it's possible. Even probable."

"Well, it doesn't seem likely to me. It happens all the time without anyone getting murdered because of it."

"You're right there, Purvy. Every girl who slips sure doesn't get murdered. So I figure it must have had a kind of extra meaning in relation to something else. It *threatened* something."

This made sense, which Purvy had to admit to himself, although it amounted to nothing more, really, than a guess. Purvy didn't want to make any guesses about anything, so he was silent.

"You want to know what I found in the registrations at Sylvan Green, Purvy?"

"No."

"I can understand how you feel. I didn't want to know myself, as a matter of fact, and I wouldn't blame anyone else for not wanting to. It was necessary in my case, though, because of my job, and it's necessary in yours because you're in a spot and ought to know what to watch out for. Besides, you might be able to help me. You helped me once, and you might be able to do it again."

"I don't see how I can help you any more than I already have."

"Maybe you'll see after I tell you. First, though, I've got to tell you what I found out at Sylvan Green. Who was there during the time I checked." Lonnie leaned back and closed his eyes, as if it were easier to say in the dark what needed saying. "Guy Butler," he said, "Rex Tye. Ellis Kuder." Purvy felt an instantaneous and hysterical compulsion to scream a protest, to dispel at once from the mind of Lonnie Womber any suspicion it might hold of the three whose names were mentioned. It was untenable, that was all. It was a monstrous distortion of the way everything had always been and ought always to be. Fellows you knew and liked sometimes got into trouble, and might even have the bad luck to get a girl pregnant, but they didn't murder her for that reason, or for any reason, or anyone at all for any reason whatever.

"Lots of people from Rutherford go to Sylvan Green," he said. "It's good bass fishing there."

"I know. I was there myself a couple years ago. I found another name I recognized, to be truthful, but it was a fellow who doesn't fit. No use mentioning him or considering him, in my opinion. He's got kids older than you or me, must be close to seventy himself, and had his wife with him besides."

"Just the same, I don't believe it was Guy or Rex or Ellis."

"What you mean is, you don't *want* to believe it, and neither do I. The point is, Purvy, you and I aren't in a position to be generous. Not I because I've got a job. Not you because you talked too much. There's a murderer around here, and he's watching and listening, and he's probably filled with a bigger fear than we can imagine, and he knows that you got a glimpse of him in that little park, something distinctive that sticks in your mind and may mean something to you if you ever get it straight, and he keeps wondering if you ever will. He wonders and wonders, and he wishes you were dead, and he may try to arrange it for you."

Purvy squirmed and wanted again to scream.

"Goddamn it, Lonnie, I wish you wouldn't try to scare me."

"You ought to be scared, Purvy. You ought to be running scared until this is settled. I admit running scared gets wearisome after a while, and so I thought you might be willing to do something for me that could hurry things up, if we're lucky."

"What could I do?"

"It's simple. You could tell a little lie."

"A lie about what?"

"You could make out that you've remembered what it was you saw in that little park. The thing that's been itching you. You could spread it around that you're damn well sure who it was that met Avis Pisano there the night she was murdered, but you'd have to make it plain at the same time that you hadn't told me or anyone else, and hadn't made up your mind to tell. You could say that it's just impossible for you to believe that this person would do a terrible thing like murdering the girl, and you don't want to make a lot of trouble for him that he doesn't deserve."

"No!" Purvy jumped to his feet, and this time his voice did skid upward until he was close to screaming. "Damn it, Lonnie, I won't do it, and that's all there is to it!"

"Well, it would probably make the murderer take a crack at you, and I don't blame you for being afraid to do it, even though I'd have you watched all the time to prevent his getting away with anything."

"All right. I'm afraid, and I admit it, but it's not only that. Guy and Rex and Ellis are friends of mine, and I don't intend to play any dirty tricks on them."

"One of them may not be your friend, Purvy. One of them may be the deadliest enemy you've ever had or are likely to have."

"Well, you're just trying to mix me up so I'll agree to do it, and I'm not going to listen to another damn word."

"All right, Purvy." Lonnie sighed and stood up. "You're not obliged to do it, and there's no way I can make you if you don't want to. I intend to find out which one it was, one way or another, but I just thought this might be a good trick to do it faster. Bear in mind what I told you, though, Purvy. Run scared. Keep running scared."

Purvy didn't answer. He got out of the office, out of the jail, and headed for town. He was scared, all right, and he was all mixed up besides, and the whole world seemed like that dark room at night when he was a kid.

# CHAPTER 15

Guy Butler slept and later wakened. He had not slept long or heavily, and no time seemed to have passed. The soft light still burned beside the bed. Phyllis Bagby, raised on one elbow, looked down at him with tenderness in her eyes and a kind of conflicting bitterness tucking the corners of her mouth and turning them down. Even so, her face was lovely, with a thin, fastidious sensuality in it.

"I ought to hate you," she said.

"So you should," he agreed.

"You treat me like a whore."

"I make love to you, and you make love to me. We treat each other like whores."

"It's different with me. I *feel* love when I make it. You don't."

"All right. Have it your own way."

"You're very agreeable, aren't you?"

"I don't want to quarrel with you, if that's what you mean."

"Why do you treat me with contempt?"

"I'm not aware that I do. Is making love to you contemptuous?"

"Perhaps not. It depends. At least, the way things are, it's contemptible."

"In that case, I'd better quit. If you don't want me to make love to you, you only have to say so."

"I do want it. That's why I accept it, even though I know you despise me."

"I don't despise you. I like you better, I think, than anyone else on earth."

"That's very nice to hear, but I don't believe it."

"All right. If I tell you the truth, you don't believe it, so there is obviously no use in saying anything at all."

"If you cared anything about me, you wouldn't have stayed away so long."

"I stayed away because I didn't think it was wise to come."

"Why did you come tonight, then?"

"I didn't intend to. I came because I needed you, and felt compelled."

"Now that I have satisfied your need, I suppose you will stay away for another long time."

"Maybe a long time. Maybe forever."

"Depending on whether you can make that rich little bitch up on the ridge. Is that it?"

"I don't want to make her. I want to marry her."

"Get out! Goddamn you, Guy, get out of my bed!"

"Do you really want me to?"

"No."

"I didn't think so."

"God," she said. "Oh, God."

She lay down on her back beside him and stared up at the ceiling with hot, dry eyes. He reached over and placed his left hand flat on her belly, and she trembled for a moment and grew rigidly still.

"You're a rotten bastard," she said.

"That's right," he said. "I am."

"It gives you pleasure to tear my insides apart."

"I don't know. Maybe it does."

"Bastard. Rotten, sadistic bastard."

"Maybe worse," he said. "Maybe murderer."

Her body trembled again, a sudden spasm that shook her and sickened her and left her lying rigid as before.

"Guy! What are you saying?"

"You sound frightened, Phyll. Do you think I could commit a murder?"

"I don't know. Sometimes I think you might do anything."

"What do you think a murderer feels when he murders? Terror? Anger? A kind of enormous exhilaration and assurance of immunity?"

"I don't know. I don't want to talk about it."

"But I do. I want to talk about it, Phyll. I want you to tell me if you think I might have killed the girl who was found outside of town in the slough. Lonnie Womber thinks so."

"Why in God's name should he think you killed her?"

"I didn't say he thinks I did. I said he thinks I might have."

"You're joking. This is another one of your damned distorted vicious jokes."

"No. No joke. Lonnie thinks so, and he has reasons. He found out that Avis Pisano worked at Sylvan Green last summer. He found out that I was there. Avis was pregnant, and she came to Rutherford, and someone killed her here, or near here, and even Lonnie can add that up and get an answer."

"Was it yours, Guy? Was the child yours?"

"If there were a possibility, do you think I would tell you the truth?"

"No. I think you would lie and lie, but I would believe you anyhow, because I'd want to."

"Then there is no point in your asking or my answering." She did not move. How could one be so quiet, she wondered, with such terror and anguish within? And what kind of woman was she whose terror sprang, not from what he was or might have done, but from his deadly peril? Whose anguish issued from the knowledge that he had possibly given a child to someone else, and not to her?

"You and your goddamned crippled hand," she said. "You think, because you have lost something, that you have the right to destroy everyone else."

He didn't answer. From his face, which did not change, there was no way of telling that he had ever heard. After a minute, perhaps two, he sat up on the edge of the bed with his back to her and lit a cigarette, which he took from a pack on a table beside him. She sat up also, leaning forward and laying her cheek against his back.

"I'll tear my tongue out," she said. "Say the word, Guy, I'll tear my rotten tongue out."

\* \* \* \*

Rex Tye came downstairs quietly and would have gone directly out the front door if his mother had not spoken to him. He turned and saw her standing in the entrance to the living room.

"Yes, Mother?" he said.

"Are you going out?"

"If you don't mind."

"Of course not, darling. I should have thought, however, that you'd tell me good-bye."

Against the brighter light of the living room, she looked impeccable and gracious, the light glancing from her hair. In spite of the substance of her words, there was not the slightest sound of reproach in her voice. In his, when he answered, was no tinge of animus. They were both controlled, beautifully mannered, meticulous experts in making things seem other than they were.

"I'm sorry, Mother. I was thinking of something else."

"Yes. Poor darling. No wonder that you're distressed. Are you in a hurry?"

"Not particularly. Why?"

"I thought you might come into the living room and talk with me for a few minutes."

"All right, Mother. If you wish."

He followed her into the living room and sat down on a period chair with tapestry covered seat and back. He sat forward on the chair with his knees together and his hands resting on his knees. In his prim posture, his pale curls reflecting the light, he looked, she thought, like a young boy who had miraculously retained his grace while growing much too fast, and she felt, looking at him, a cold intensification of anger that in no way showed, not for him, but for those who transgressed against him. She thought of it as precisely that. Transgression. She wondered if he could possibly have been seduced and soiled by the vile girl who had come here to Rutherford to die, which was execrably bad taste on her part, and she had vividly a sudden revolting vision of hot entangled flesh. Closing her eyes, as if the vision were external and could thus be evaded, she surrendered herself, without ever knowing if the vision were valid or not, to a delicately savage satisfaction that the girl was dead. She did not feel for an instant, however, that Rex might have killed her. More than that, she did not for an instant feel that anyone else could seriously entertain such a suspicion.

"If you're in trouble," she said, "I wish you would let me help you."

"Trouble, Mother? I'm in no trouble."

"Please don't try to evade me, darling. Sheriff Womber has been talking to you, hasn't he?"

"He wanted to ask me a few questions, that's all. This girl who was killed worked as a waitress at Sylvan Green last summer. I knew her slightly, of course, as did practically everyone there. It's simply routine in these things to ask questions of everyone in the least connected, Mother."

"Nevertheless, it is not fair of Sheriff Womber to involve you publicly. People talk, you know. They imagine all sorts of things that are not true."

"I don't think I've been harmed, Mother."

"No? Perhaps you are far too innocent and generous. After all, this girl was pregnant."

"I know that. Everyone does."

"Then you must know, as everyone does, that you are contaminated by the least contact with this sordid affair."

"I don't feel contaminated, Mother."

"I wonder if you are fully aware of its significance. Don't you care at all if you are suspected of having been responsible for the miserable girl's condition?"

"The truth is, I don't."

"Really? That's very admirable, I'm sure. Are you also indifferent to being virtually accused of murder? Surely you understand the line of thinking that connects the two."

"Damn it, Mother. I've been accused of nothing."

"You needn't swear, darling." Just perceptibly, her mouth turned down in the briefest, slightest expression of distaste. Her selective mind was violated again by the intrusion of the vision of passion. "How do you expect to be accepted by a family like the Haigs when you permit yourself to be associated, even innocently, with such a vile crime?"

"I didn't permit it, Mother. It just happened. One can't really be expected to anticipate the result of every casual relationship or meeting, and I'm sure my innocence is apparent to the Haigs. Especially to Lauren. They are not nearly so bigoted as you seem to think."

"Am I to infer from this that *I'm* considered bigoted?"

"Not at all, Mother. You know I didn't mean that."

"I'm relieved." She smiled at him coolly, again disturbed by the fleshly vision, and she said suddenly, quite casually, "Tell me truthfully, darling, did you take that dreadful girl to bed?"

If he was in the least disconcerted by the blunt question, which was unlike anything he might have expected from her, he did not show it. He was, as a matter of fact, so used to lying to her, living the lies when they were unexpressed, that he was able to tell promptly and naturally the one now necessary.

"Of course not," he said. "I guess that's why I'm unable to feel especially concerned."

He stood up then and crossed to the chair in which she sat facing him. Bending, he kissed her cheek.

"Good-night, Mother. I'm sorry if I've caused you any distress."

"Where are you going?"

"I don't know, really. Just out. I may go to the hotel for a while."

He went out into the hall then, and she sat unmoving and listened for the sound of the front door closing behind him. It was her special terror that every closed door between them was a symbol and a prophecy. Hearing the sound, the door closing, she began at once to listen for its opening.

* * * *

Bernie Huggins wondered how far it would be advisable, or safe, to go with Ellis Kuder. Bernie was naturally curious and would have been willing to set up a couple of drinks on the house in exchange for a little inside info, but Ellis was so withdrawn and sullen that chances for any kind of understanding didn't look so good, and as a matter of fact, in

Bernie's opinion, Ellis was a mean son of a bitch by nature and a fellow you couldn't afford to trifle with. He'd been sitting at the bar for all of a half hour now, and in all that time he hadn't said a word except the name of his drink when he wanted service, and when Bernie had lingered a few minutes across the mahogany to indicate that he was receptive to any friendly gesture, Ellis had ignored him and made it pretty plain that he wished Bernie would get the hell about his business. Well, if that was the way Ellis wanted it, it sure wasn't any skin off Bernie's tail, but Bernie knew one thing, all right, and what he knew was that if he was on the spot Ellis was on, suspected of getting a girl in trouble and then killing her to avoid the consequences, he'd damn well be trying to give a better impression of his character than Ellis was giving.

Of course, there wasn't anything certain about Ellis and the girl. He'd just been at that lousy resort hotel at the right time, or wrong time, that was all, and apparently Guy Butler and Rex Tye had been there, too. Bernie understood that, all right. From what he could learn from the talk going round, the girl hadn't been very choosy, round heels and all that, and probably it could have been any one of a number of guys who fixed her up, but what made it look bad was that she had come to Rutherford on the train, and had been met by someone here, and, well, it simply looked like a local hero, and that's all there was to it.

The way Bernie got it, neither Guy nor Rex nor Ellis could establish any alibi for the full period of time in which it was figured the murder was done, and if anyone cared for his opinion, which was free, any one of the three snotty bastards was perfectly capable of doing it if the chips were down. It wouldn't be smart to express an opinion like that, of course, because most people thought it was absolutely ridiculous to suspect Guy or Rex or Ellis of murder, though fornication might be allowed, but Bernie had been around and had seen what he had seen, and as a result he had a lot of good opinions that he was forced to keep to himself for sagacious reasons.

Another thing you had to consider, though, to be perfectly honest about it. You only had the word of Purvy Stubbs that this girl, this Avis Pisano, was met by someone at the station, and Purvy, it was well known, didn't have brains enough to pour pee out of a boot with the directions on the heel. He told this wacky story about seeing a shadow in that little park at the end of the platform, and how the girl went down there and disappeared, and it sounded a hell of a lot like a good story, or a damn lie, which Purvy wasn't above telling for effect, but in Purvy's favor was the fact that he'd told the story before the murder was discovered, when there didn't seem to be any point in telling it unless it was true. Purvy was an odd nut and might be guilty of concocting a good story after the fact, just to get a little attention, but no one could possibly contend that he was psychic or something, and able to anticipate a murder that hadn't happened. Psychic? Hell, he was barely conscious. You could just look at him now and make up your own mind, if you had any doubts. He was sitting down there at the bar, four stools from Ellis, and he was stewed to his lousy gills. He'd been getting that way the last few days, and it was unusual and peculiar, because Purvy'd always been a light drinker, just a little beer for sociability, but now he'd started drinking whisky and was about as sociable as a muskrat. You might think, to watch him, that he was the one who was on the spot, except that it was doubtful that the simpleton could whip a girl in a fair fight, let alone kill her, and it was even more doubtful, if possible, that he could put one in a condition.

Just then, as Bernie examined Purvy and reflected on his inadequacies, Ellis lifted his empty glass and set it down with a thump. Bernie jumped and cursed silently. Picking up the cue, he moved down opposite Ellis.

"Another?" he said.

Ellis nodded. Bernie fixed another and set it out. Ellis paid, and Bernie rang it up. After registering the sale, he decided that he'd give Ellis just one more chance to be sociable, just refer sort of jokingly to Ellis being inside the excitement, something like that. He tried to think of the best way to put it.

"Well," he said, "I hear you and Lonnie Womber been working together on Rutherford's murder case."

Ellis looked at him. "Do you?" he said.

"That's what I hear. Guy Butler and Rex Tye, too, for that matter. Seems like half the young guys in town knew this Avis Pisano, one way or another. Must be a shock to have someone you knew, maybe talked with and had a drink with or something, turn up murdered. What kind of girl was she, Ellis? Pretty good kid? Lot of people condemn her out of hand because of the condition she was in, but I'm not that way myself. No justice in just blaming the ones that get caught if you want my opinion."

"She was a cheap little bitch," Ellis said.

Well, Bernie was no sissy. He'd been tending bar for a long time, after all, and bartenders don't generally get softer as they get older, but it gave him a jolt, just the same, to hear Ellis come out with it like that. It was brutal, that's what it was. Whatever the girl had been, it was time to forget it now, and maybe even to tell a few lies in her favor. It didn't do any harm to lie a little for someone who was dead, and the least you could do, if you had scruples or something, was to say nothing at all.

Bernie thought all this, but he didn't say it, and consequently he said nothing. Down the bar, Purvy Stubbs had come to life. He turned his head slowly and looked up at Ellis. He seemed to be working very hard at focusing his eyes.

"I'll tell you something, though, Bernie," Ellis said. "Whoever made her, it wasn't me, and whoever killed her, it wasn't me. Remember that. I'm just telling you so you'll have it straight when you pass it over the bar."

This made Bernie hot, the implication that he was a lousy blabber-mouth, and he was fumbling around in his brain, trying to sort out the right words to tell Ellis to go to hell indirectly, when Purvy Stubbs spoke up suddenly, enunciating carefully and getting his words out with only the slightest fuzz on them.

"I remember," Purvy said clearly. "I remember what it was about the one who was waiting in the little park. What was familiar about him, I mean."

Bernie and Ellis turned to stare at him. Slowly, after adjustment, the significance of Purvy's words sank in.

"The hell you do!" Bernie said.

Purvy nodded, and Bernie and Ellis waited. Purvy's eyes still didn't appear to be focused quite properly, and he rubbed the back of a hand across them.

"Well, damn it, Purvy, speak up!" Bernie said. "Who was it?"

Purvy rubbed his hand across his eyes again. Turning his head, he looked into his glass and spoke to it.

"I don't think I ought to tell," he said. "I don't think I ought to tell anyone."

"What do you mean, you don't think you ought to tell?" Bernie sounded almost frantic. "Damn it, Purvy, do you think this is a game of button, button, who's got the button? This happens to be a murder, and you're obligated to tell anything you know that might help. Lonnie Womber gets ahold of you, you'll damn well tell, all right."

"No." Purvy still talked to the glass. "This is someone who wouldn't commit any murder, and I know it. It wouldn't be right to get him into a lot of trouble he doesn't deserve. I'm determined not to tell, and Lonnie Womber or anyone else isn't going to get me to do it."

Suddenly, he pushed the glass away and stood up and walked out of the bar. Bernie, watching him go in amazement, was about to deliver an opinion on lubberly fools in general and one in particular, but he got at that moment a glimpse of Ellis Kuder's eyes, and his mind went coldly blank to everything else.

He had seen friendlier eyes, he thought, in the head of a snake.

\* \* \* \*

Walking down Main Street, Purvy wondered why he'd done it. He hadn't intended to, but he suddenly had and now it was done. Maybe he'd done it because it had become imperative to get the whole thing over with as quickly as possible, and this seemed like the quickest way, and maybe the only way.

In the residential streets, beyond the area of light, he became aware of someone following him, and he began to trot. The one who followed began to trot also. Together, a particular distance apart, they trotted through the streets and all the way up the long slope to the ridge. Purvy had been told that people who didn't exercise much sometimes grew a kind of fatty tissue around the heart, and that it could be dangerous for that reason for them to exert themselves excessively too suddenly, and as he began to feel a developing pain in his chest, he visualized himself dropping dead, his heart smothered and stopped by the enveloping fat, but his fear of the one who followed was greater than his fear of death, and so he kept on trotting.

When he reached home at last, he closed the door behind him and locked it, but it was no barrier. The one who followed came right through the door and followed him upstairs and stood all night at the foot of his bed.

# CHAPTER 16

"Darling," he whispered. "Darling, darling."

His voice lingered and faded in Lauren's mind, repeating and repeating itself on the breath of a dying sigh. She lifted her face from the soft hollow of his throat and sought blindly for his mouth with hers. She found it and was drawn in and in to the heart of a giant heart that beat like thunder in an agony of aggressive submission. His hands were at once transgressors and supplicants, eliciting a pleasurable pain.

"Now, Curly," she said. "Now, please."

And so it was reached at last, the delicate and perilous point in the methodically projected and executed seduction at which everything was finally committed. It was the tenth night after the night Avis Pisano was murdered, and they were on a leather sofa in front of a fire in the library of the biggest house on the ridge, where the rich of Rutherford lived, and afterward they lay quietly in a suddenly shrunken world that seemed to expand and contract with the rhythm of their own deep breathing, and he was afraid. Now he must wait to see if it was consummation or abortion, lie in the shrunken world and wait for the sign, and after a while, with a kind of dreamy and assured validity in the recession of passion, she laid her fingers on his cheek and said, "I love you," and he knew that it was all right and that he had won. The world assumed again its vast design, and he in the world again his giant size. Twice he had committed himself and twice he had won, and he felt now, after the second commitment, the same sense of singing power that he had felt after the first. He was somehow removed from the measures of good and evil. He was briefly and grandly immune to danger.

Her fingers trailed away, leaving his face, and she was immediately so still, her breathing so regular, that he turned his head to look at her, thinking that she was asleep, and she had indeed the appearance of being asleep, but she wasn't. Her lashes lay in their own shadows, and a lighter shadow of sadness was on her face, and this, though he didn't know it, was because she was saying good-bye to herself, to the cool and lovely girl she had solely possessed, and now did not, and would never again. But in the sadness there was also pride, an exorbitant sense of accomplishment in having boldly done something she could not have done a little while ago, and in feeling now no other regret than the sadness itself, which was really not regret at all.

"Are you asleep?" he said.

"No."

"Are you sorry?"

"No."

'What are you thinking?"

"I'm thinking that I would like to be married. I'd like to be married very soon, if you don't mind."

"When?"

"Tomorrow. It's all in my mind, the way I want it. We will drive up to the city tomorrow evening and be married there and spend the night in a hotel, and it will be impossible for anyone to do anything to prevent it or change it."

"Who would want to prevent it?"

"Father will be angry for a while, of course, but it won't matter."

"I didn't know that your father was so opposed to me."

"He isn't, really. It's just this horrible business about the murdered girl."

"Why? Does he think I murdered her?"

He said it lightly, with an edge of bitter humor that was just sufficient to imply tolerance of a monstrous injustice, and he felt a surge of great pride that he was able to accomplish the effect so perfectly. Oh, he was enormously daring and clever, and he was perfectly capable of manipulating to the attainment of his own triumph the very threats of his own destruction. Only a very exceptional person, of course, could refer so quietly, with such an admirable implication of absurdity, to his own engrossing guilt.

"No, of course not," she said. "Please don't joke about such a terrible thing. You know how fathers are. It's just that you are innocently involved, however slightly, by the fact that you knew her, or at least had some contact with her, at Sylvan Green last summer. It's perfectly ridiculous, darling, but I'm afraid you must consider yourself tainted."

"Well, I can't blame your father, actually. After all, the damn girl was pregnant, and I was at Sylvan Green at a time to have accomplished it. Considering that she came here to see someone and was apparently killed here by that someone, this is at least enough to make me a subject of suspicion."

"Don't talk like that. Father only takes the foolish position that you were unpardonably indiscreet in not avoiding something you could not possibly anticipate. After a while he will see how absurd he has been."

"I'm surprised that he permits me to come here now."

"To tell the truth, he did make something of an issue of it, and I became quite angry. When I became angry, he conceded at once. I am hardly ever angry about anything, and I think it actually frightened him a little. Do you want me to tell you something strange? Before Father took such an intolerable position, I was not at all convinced that I loved you or wanted to continue seeing you, but then, almost at once, I was absolutely certain and was determined to have you in spite of any opposition."

He had an almost irresistible compulsion to laugh, to laugh and laugh in high, hysterical glee at the perversity of factors that might have ruined him but worked in his favor instead. He was truly the beneficiary of an incredible collaboration of daring and ingenuity and miraculous luck.

"Are you sure?" he said, inviting with a kind of arrogant bravado a retraction of the cardinal commitment upon which everything depended.

"Yes," she said. "I think I've never been so sure of anything before."

And this was true. She had never before made a significant decision which required on her part the assumption of a positive position, and now that she had made one, she was filled with a strange assurance and a disproportionate sense of excitement. Twisting on the leather sofa to face him, she held him tightly in fierce possessiveness, her mind and body responding again with aggressive submission to the resumed stroking of his hands.

"When shall we leave?" he said. "For the city, I mean."

"It had better be late. Come for me about eight. Mother and Father have a dinner engagement and will be gone then. I'll have to take a bag, and it will be much easier to get away if they're not here. It should only take about an hour and a half to get to the city."

"Eight," he said. "Eight o'clock."

The name of the hour was like a pulse, beating in time with his stroking hands, as if the name and the hands were themselves measuring seconds. Somehow, now that the time for their departure was established, the short stretch of hours between now and then became in his mind a cumulative threat, a space of time in which all danger and all possibility of disaster were gathered. Now the remaining perilous imperative was to survive by courage and cleverness for less than one more full day.

And in that diminished day, in order to secure the future, it would be necessary to kill a clown. He had thought and thought about it very carefully, and he had been deterred only by the added danger to himself, but there was surely greater danger in trusting the silence of the clown, who had seen too much by chance, which was the clown's bad luck, and even in waiting this long there had been an appalling calculated risk.

He was conscious of Lauren's quickened breathing. Her body was beginning to tremble again. Stroking her gently, he reviewed in his mind the way he would kill Purvy Stubbs.

# CHAPTER 17

By six o'clock the next evening, Purvy was drunk. He was not obviously or offensively drunk, but had merely achieved a sufficient degree of absorption to reconcile him to his problems and to enable him the better to tolerate them, if not to cope with them. At that time, at six o'clock, he went into the dining room of the Division Hotel and ordered baked pork chops with whipped potatoes and applesauce for dinner, but he was not hungry and only picked at the food. After twenty minutes had passed, he got up and went out of the dining room and across the lobby into the taproom. Established on a stool, he ordered whisky.

"Purvy," said Bernie Huggins, "what the hell's the matter with you?"

"There's nothing at all the matter with me, Bernie," Purvy said. "Why do you ask?"

"Well, you came in here and got plastered before dark, which is too early in the day in the winter for anyone to be plastered, and it's something, besides, that you've never done before. All the time I've known you, you never drank anything but beer, and damn little of that, and now all of a sudden you switch to whisky. In my opinion, something's on your mind, and I know what it is."

"If you know what it is, why the hell are you asking?"

"All right, all right. Be as pig-headed as you please."

"Well, I know what you're after, Bernie. Maybe I'm not as dumb as you think, or as drunk either. You're trying to get me to tell you what I saw down there in that little park at the station, and I'm determined not to do it."

Bernie took a deep breath and a swipe at the bar. He looked at Purvy for several seconds with an expression that was meant to be disconcerting, and was. Purvy squirmed on his stool and drank some of his whisky.

"You want to know what I think, Purvy?" Bernie asked.

"Not particularly," Purvy said. "I can't say I've got a hell of a lot of interest in what you think."

"Is that so? Well, I'll just tell you, anyhow, Purvy, and I'll give you a little tip besides, which is that a lot of other fellows think the same thing, and it's been getting passed up and down the bar. What I think, I think you didn't see anything at all in that little park, not a single solitary damn thing, and you just told that cock and bull story to get a little attention for yourself."

"Why would I do a crazy thing like that?"

"I just told you. To get attention. Lots of nuts do that sort of thing, and you can read in the papers almost any day where some nut somewhere has done it. Especially in the big cases. People seeing things and making fake confessions and all sorts of things like that, just to cash in on the excitement and publicity and all. It's psychological, that's what it is."

Purvy's indignation was impressive. Even Bernie was impressed. As Purvy swelled slowly, like a frog about to burst into song, Bernie had for a moment an uneasy feeling that he might actually explode and splatter all over the taproom.

"By God, Bernie," he Said, "I've never had such big lies told about me in my life before, and that's the truth. You ought to be ashamed of yourself. Here I've been, sweating this out, and worrying myself sick over it, and wishing and wishing I'd never been near that damn station platform that night, and all the time you and a lot of other guys been thinking and spreading around that I just made it all up to get people to look at me and listen to me and crap like that. Well, I don't mind telling you I don't care if you never look at me or speak to me again, Bernie Huggins, and the truth is, the way I feel now, I'd a lot rather you wouldn't."

Purvy finished his whisky in a gulp, and slipped off the stool. His knees buckled a little, and he grasped the edge of the bar and pulled himself erect. On the other side of the bar, Bernie watched him with some evidence of concern. As a matter of fact, Bernie had a sort of soft spot for Purvy and was feeling contrite for having insulted him. He didn't object to making Purvy sore, so far as that went, but he didn't want to make him sore *permanently*, that was the difference, and he'd only accused Purvy of being a damn liar and publicity hog because Purvy had been so pig-headed about keeping to himself whatever it was he knew.

"Look, Purvy," he said. "You don't need to go off in a huff. Chances are I've exaggerated things a little."

Purvy turned carefully away and got himself pointed, after a moment, toward the entrance to the lobby.

"You said what you said, and I heard you," he said. "Kindly do me the favor of going to hell, Bernie."

"Okay, Purvy. If that's the way you feel about it. Incidentally, where are *you* going?"

"None of your business," Purvy said. "None at all. I only tell my business to my friends."

"Don't be like that, Purvy. I'm your friend, and you know it."

"I'm damned if I do. My friends don't call me a liar directly and a nut by inference."

"I didn't infer that you're a nut."

"Yes, you did, Bernie. It was perfectly clear what you meant, and it's too late to try to wiggle out of it now. I may never come into your crummy taproom again."

Having delivered himself of this threat, which was not particularly alarming to Bernie or anyone else, he went out through the hotel lobby onto Main Street and turned in the direction of the railroad station. It was very cold, probably about ten degrees below freezing, and he walked along at a pretty good clip for someone carrying a load of whisky, his hands shoved into his topcoat pockets and the too-short skirt of the coat flapping around his knees. The cold air sobered him some, which was good in a way and bad in another. It cleared his head and permitted him to think better, which was good, but it also made him conscious again of someone following him, which was bad. It didn't do a bit of good to tell himself that it was all his imagination and nothing more, that it was simply impossible for someone to follow him every place he went and stand all night at the foot of his bed, for it was precisely his imagination that made the follower so frightening and so perfectly capable of the impossible.

What Purvy intended to do now, first thing, was watch the seven-o-five come in and go out. Not really first thing though, because it was only a little past six-thirty, maybe six-thirty-five, and the really first thing he'd do would be to go down to the restaurant and have a cup of coffee with Pheeb Keeley. Maybe Pheeb poked a little fun at him about girls and trains, but he liked her and got a kick out of talking with her just the same, and she certainly wasn't any goddamned smart-aleck like big-mouth Bernie Huggins, who'd accused him of being a liar and a nut. It was true that she sometimes referred to him as an odd ball, but that was different, the way she said it and the meaning and all, and the fact was, she seemed to have a kind of admiration for him.

Well, he'd have a cup of coffee with Pheeb, and watch the seven-o-five come in and go out, and after that he'd wait around in the restaurant, or go read the magazines at the newsstand in the main waiting room, until the seven-thirty-eight freight came through. The freight was one of the trains he liked best, a big 4-8-4 steam job, and it didn't stop at the passenger station, of course, but went thundering right past on the farthest pair of rails over from the platform, the very last pair, with ten other pairs between. This was too far removed to suit Purvy, and it was his habit to walk across the rails, a few minutes before the freight arrived, clear across beyond all the tracks, and it was then the most exciting experience it was possible to have, standing beside the rails as close as he dared in the great white glare of the headlight as the engine swept down upon him and past him with pounding drives and thunderous wheels in an overwhelming assault of sound that filled and rocked the world. It was especially exciting in winter, when it was dark early, best of all as the great light passed and the night closed in upon him and the rushing cars. By thunder and darkness deified, he was Lord God Stubbs astride a spinning sphere.

Phyllis Bagby saw him when he left the hotel. She could tell that he was drunk, and she knew that he was drunk because he was afraid. Perhaps she knew this so surely because she was afraid herself, and was therefore sensitized to the look and feel of fear in others. She had been waiting for quite a long time for Purvy to leave. Having seen him enter the hotel over an hour earlier, she had been sitting very quietly ever since in a straight chair by the door of her beauty parlor, waiting and watching and thinking of things she did not wish to think about. It was quite chilly in the room in which she sat, for she had turned down the thermostat for the night, but she was not aware of the cold. Wearing a mouton coat and matching mouton hat, she sat in the chair and looked down and across the street at an angle to the door of the hotel.

She did not know exactly why she waited, except that it was imperative. Purvy Stubbs was in danger, of course. Deadly danger. This was a feeling that had grown within her to the stature of conviction, and her own fear had grown in ratio to her certainty of Purvy's danger. It was peculiar, the quality of her fear, something she had not analyzed and had not really wished to analyze, but she knew that it was somehow a perversion and unclean. And now, sitting in the dark cold room in the straight chair, she deliberately considered it and tried to understand it, and the perversion was, of course, that she was not so much afraid for Purvy, for what might happen to him, as for what might happen as a consequence to one who possibly threatened him.

*Guy*, she thought. *God, don't let it be Guy!*

She was not accustomed to praying, and she was not really praying now. It was merely a blind and undirected cry for help in traditional terms. Anyhow, she did not really believe it was Guy. Not Guy who had killed the girl and left her body in the dry slough and was now a threat to the bumbling, kindly fellow who had seen him by chance in damning circumstances and was too loyal, or too stupid, to relieve himself of danger simply by telling what he knew. She did not believe it was Guy, but she didn't *know*, and the doubt was there in her mind, the perverted fear.

Phyllis was no fool. She had been thinking for herself and doing for herself for more years than she liked to remember, and in the conduct of her affairs, sometimes questionable by proper standards, she had developed a shrewdness that was based essentially upon a sure feeling for character, the ability to judge what someone else might or might not be capable of doing. Her judgment was not infallible, of course, as she had learned empirically, but it worked on the whole with satisfying accuracy. This shrewdness, the feeling for character, she had applied to the murder of Avis Pisano, who had killed her, and this was the problem primarily of the three young men of Rutherford who had been incriminated by circumstances. Guy and Rex Tye and Ellis Kuder. In her mind she examined with a kind of fearful thoroughness every slightest thing she knew about them, each in turn and over and over again, and after a while, though any one of the three was capable of his own atrocities in his own way and own time, she began to believe that *only* one of them was capable of this particular atrocity in the time and circumstances of its commission. Only one.

This she believed, but she did not *know*.

So she thought the prayer that was not really a prayer.

So she sat in the cold room of her beauty parlor and waited and watched, and Purvy Stubbs came out of the Division Hotel, drunk with fear and bourbon.

Getting up at once, she went outside and started after Purvy, about a half block behind and on the opposite side of the street. Purvy walked rapidly, in spite of his condition, his topcoat flapping around his knees. It was soon apparent that he was going to the railroad station, which she had anticipated, as anyone would have anticipated who knew Purvy at all, and she wondered again why she had waited for him to leave the hotel, why she was now following him, and all she knew, as she had known before, was that it was somehow imperative and must be done. Perhaps in her mind, below compulsion and reason and perverted fear, was the obscure understanding that the time for the attack on Purvy was necessarily now, or very soon, and that the place was logically the dark surrounding area of the station, where he went by habit, in strange and tenacious desire, to watch the trains come in. It was not in the hope of saving him that she followed, nor in the positive need to know the identity of his danger; it was in the greater hope and darker need to know for once and all who his danger was not.

Ahead of her, Purvy turned the corner onto the dark, narrow street that ran in front of the station, and she increased her pace in pursuit, but when she reached the corner and turned it herself, Purvy had already vanished. Accelerating her pace still more, rising on her toes to keep her high heels from rapping too sharply on the rough walk, she hurried down to the entrance and looked in through the high window in the door just in time to see Purvy going out the exit onto the platform on the other side of the building. She stood quietly in the narrow street, wondering what she should do. Purvy was going down the platform, she assumed, to the station restaurant. She did not want to follow him there, nor would it be advisable to wait in the waiting room, and so she went, after considering the problem, along the front of the station to its southeast corner, turning there and walking toward the south end of the platform. Slipping quickly along the edge of yellow light, she entered the little park and sat down on the bench among the whispering Junipers.

Now she began to feel the cold. Clenching her teeth to prevent their chattering, huddling in her mouton coat, she stared at the door of the restaurant into which Purvy had gone, and she thought that she was truly engaged in incredible idiocy. Obviously she could not follow Purvy indefinitely, watch him constantly, and chances were that she would gain nothing from her vigil tonight except a bad cold, or possibly pneumonia. It would be more sensible by far to tell Lonnie Womber of her suspicions frankly, which would relieve her of whatever guilt might be assumed in silence, and Lonnie could then do as he pleased about it, something or nothing according to his judgment.

Thinking of Lonnie, she knew for an instant the greatest terror of her life when he spoke to her suddenly. When the terror subsided, leaving her weak and near hysteria, she was aware that she was standing, ready to run, but she could never afterward remember rising from the bench.

"Oh, Christ!" she said.

"I'm sorry if I frightened you," Lonnie said. "I was here when you came. I've been standing behind you and wondering what in hell you could possibly be up to."

"I followed Purvy Stubbs here. He's in the restaurant now. At least I assume he is."

"He's there, all right. Went in just before you came. Why are you following Purvy?"

"I don't know, really. It just seemed imperative."

"Because he talked out of turn? Because you think a murderer may take a crack at him?"

"I suppose so."

"What could you possibly do about it if he did?"

"I don't know. Scream, perhaps. Frighten him off."

"Possibly. Possibly get yourself murdered, too."

"I hadn't thought of that."

"It's something to think of. You'd better let me handle this, Miss Bagby. It's my job. Believe me, I'm fully aware that Purvy may be attacked. I've even got a good idea of where and when it may happen."

"Where? Here at the station?"

He looked at her for a while without speaking, plainly considering the wisdom of answering her directly.

"If I tell you," he said finally, "will you go home and mind your own business?"

"Yes."

"All right. See that last pair of rails over there? Within the next hour a freight will pass on them. Purvy has a habit of crossing the tracks and standing on the other side to watch the freight pass. God knows why. God knows why Purvy does half the crazy things he does when it comes to trains. Anyhow, the freight itself will be between Purvy and the station. Behind him will be nothing but a few old sheds and a high board fence. Everyone who knows Purvy knows he does this regularly. Including the murderer. I figure it will happen there and then, if it happens at all. On the other side of the freight when it passes through."

"How can you be sure?"

"I can't. I just think so because it seems to be the best possible time and place."

"If you think so, why don't you tell Purvy not to go across the tracks?"

"Because I want him to go. I need him for bait. If you think that's pretty risky, you're right. It is. If you think I'm a heel for letting him, you may be right, too. I won't argue the point. Incidentally, would you mind telling me why you've concerned yourself with Purvy's trouble?"

"I know Purvy. He comes to talk with me. I like him."

"Is that all?"

"What else could there be?"

"You're frightened, Miss Bagby. I'm willing to bet that it's not entirely for Purvy. Or even mostly."

"I don't see how you could possibly get such an idea."

"Don't you? Well, it doesn't matter. You better go away now. Go home, or to a movie, or anywhere at all that's away from this."

She stared at him for a moment, at the pale blur of his face in the darkness, and then she turned and walked away, colder under the mouton than even the cold night could make her.

Lonnie stayed on in the little park until the seven-o-five had arrived and departed. Then he crossed the tracks and stood in pitch darkness inside one of the old sheds on the far side.

\* \* \* \*

At the station, Purvy went through the waiting room, as usual, and down the platform to the restaurant. Ahead of him was the dark little park of whispering Junipers, but now he saw no shadow among shadows, and this was now to be expected, of course, for the shadow was behind him. He hurried into the warmth behind steamed windows and sat on a stool at the oval counter. Inside the oval, Phoebe Keeley approached, sniffing audibly the last few steps.

"Purvy," she said, "are you drunk?"

"No, I'm not, Pheeb," Purvy said. "I had a few drinks at the hotel, but I'm not drunk."

"I didn't know you drank, Purvy."

"I don't much, to tell the truth. Usually I just take a little beer to be sociable."

"It sure as hell isn't beer I'm smelling now."

"Well, I've got onto whisky lately, for some reason or other."

"If you want to know the truth, you smell like you'd been taking a bath in it, and what's more, if you aren't drunk now, you have been, and there's no use denying it."

"All right, Pheeb, all right. Let up on it, will you? If you're bound and determined to have your own way, I don't intend to argue about it."

"No need to get huffy, Purvy. It's your own business if you want to have a few drinks, and what I don't see is why you feel like you've got to deny it or be so damn sensitive about it. You like a cup of coffee?"

"I sure would, Pheeb. Thanks."

She drew the cup from an urn and put it in front of him. It was too hot to drink right away, so he spent a while smelling it. Phoebe spent the same while waiting on a couple who were waiting on the train. The service completed, she returned to Purvy.

"How's the murder coming, Purvy?" she said.

"What?" Purvy said, slopping over into his saucer. "What you mean, Pheeb, how's the murder coming?"

"Just what I said. How's it coming?"

"Damn it, Pheeb, I don't know any more about it than anyone else. Why ask me?"

"Well, that's not the way I heard it. I heard you saw something down at the end of the platform that night that's going to help Lonnie Womber turn up the one who did it in no time. It's all over about how you recognized someone who met her or something."

"I haven't told Lonnie Womber a thing, and I don't intend to."

"Why not?"

"Just because someone met her doesn't mean he killed her. Damn it, Pheeb, there's no law against meeting someone at the station."

"That's not your worry. Let him explain it to Lonnie."

"That's the trouble, Pheeb. Maybe he couldn't explain it to Lonnie's satisfaction. I've read how it happened lots of times how an innocent person couldn't explain away something that looked bad for him. Besides, to tell the truth, I'm not absolutely sure who it was. I think I know, but I'm not absolutely sure. Anyhow, I couldn't prove it."

Phoebe was looking at him with incredulity in her face, and maybe just a touch of the admiration he thought he sometimes detected.

"For God's sake, Purvy, haven't you got any sense whatever? You can't keep something like this to yourself for such a crazy reason as that. You ever stopped to think it might be dangerous?"

Her expression changed, and she started looking at him as if he were already dead, a compromise between horror and pity. Suddenly her eyes slithered uneasily to the door to the platform, and he had a terrified feeling that the murderer had come soundlessly into the room from out of the yellow light, bearing upon himself some terrible mark of identification, and was at that moment standing motionless behind him.

Purvy's head swam, and he had a sensation of falling. The warmth of the restaurant was restoring the effect of the whisky, that's what it was. Putting his head in his hands, he held it.

Phoebe, watching him, was beginning to feel apprehensive. She wondered if the poor guy was going to pass out in the restaurant, and she was about to suggest that he step outside onto the platform and breathe some fresh air when half a dozen fellows from town came in and sat down in a row at the counter. They were fresh guys, the kind who were always making wisecracks and these remarks with a kind of double meaning that they thought were just too damn clever, and they started in at it right away, one after the other, and it required all of Phoebe's attention and skill to handle the situation. She knew how to handle cheap guys like these, though, guys who couldn't have raised ten bucks among themselves, and she did it with a fine and scornful thoroughness. In the meanwhile, Purvy held his head and breathed the hot scent of coffee and was forgotten.

At seven-o-five, the local arrived on time, and he got up and went out and stood beside the door. The conductor came down and stood beside the porter at the bottom of the steps to one of the coaches, and Purvy had a crazy notion all at once that this was the beginning of something that had already happened, that Avis Pisano would descend in a moment to the rough bricks washed with dirty yellow light, while in the park among the Junipers a shadow waited and cursed his luck. But no one at all actually descended from the coach. Two passengers came out of the station and boarded it, and the local labored on. Purvy, his head clearer again in the cold, could hear the loud voices of the wise guys in the restaurant. They ought to be ashamed, he thought, to talk to Pheeb the way they did. He didn't think it was right and didn't want to listen to it, and so he decided he'd go up to the waiting room and take a leak and look at the picture magazines at the newsstand.

Relieved, thumbing slick pages, he began to feel sleepy. He wished he could take the magazines over to one of the hard oak benches, but the newsstand operator didn't permit anyone to take the magazines away, and in fact he sometimes got snotty about anyone's looking at them at all. Replacing the magazine on the rack, Purvy went over and sat down on a bench near the doors to the platform, and it was quite warm in the waiting room, though not so warm as it had been in the restaurant, and the soft clatter of the telegraph in the agent's office was a musical and lulling sound, like the sound of a summer day, and even the stern oak bench was magically affected and wonderfully soft.

With a start, some time later, Purvy awoke to the long whistle of the seven-thirty-eight freight. He was on his feet in an instant, his rising accomplished with the opening of his eyes, and seconds later he was on his way across the platform and the ten pairs of shining rails. His response to the whistle was reflexive and excessive. When he crossed the last rail and stood waiting, facing north, the big light of the 4-8-4 was still far up the line.

The light swept down. He was assailed and blinded by the great white light. In a maximum of exhilarating thunder, with flashes of fire and roar of steam, the giant locomotive passed. Darkness rushed in where light had been, and suddenly Purvy was caught in the suction of the spinning wheels, possessed and drawn toward the center of sound and terror. Sickened and strengthened by fear of death, he set his bulk and heaved it back and around and forward again in a powerful continuity of motion that he would not ordinarily have been capable of. Through the coarse thick sound-fabric of rattle and roar ran the brief bright thread of a scream.

The cars ran by into the night. Box cars, flat cars, gondolas. Eventually the caboose. In the vast comparative silence that settled, Purvy kept company with the lifeless substance of the shadow that had stood by his bed and had tried to push him under the train.

With the murderer, and with Lonnie Womber.

Lonnie's shout had gone unheard in the thunder of wheels and the nearer piercing scream. His gun, which was in his hand, he had not needed to use. Unable to save Purvy, who had saved himself, he was at least immediately present to give comfort.

Putting an arm around Purvy's shoulders, he said softly, "It's all right, Purvy. It's all right."

But it wasn't. Purvy knew this perfectly well. It would never be all right.

*Now*, he thought with a clear and definitive sadness that would never quite end, *it is entirely ruined. I shall never feel the excitement and godliness again.*

# CHAPTER 18

As the evening passed. Time changed its pace. After seven it quickly became eight, and after eight it eventually became eight-thirty.

At first she was not excessively disturbed. She assured herself in the beginning of the long drag between the hour and the half-hour that he had certainly only been delayed and would arrive at any moment, but then, as she waited and waited and he did not come, she became slowly convinced that she had been seduced and jilted in the perpetration of a monstrous joke, and that he would not come at all. She felt for herself a great pity, for her corrupted and abandoned body a terrible grief.

But these did not last either, neither the pity nor the grief, and she was possessed instead by anger and shame and hatred, the easily attained antitheses of love. Standing in the hall beside the packed bag that she had carried downstairs immediately after the departure of her parents, she watched the long hand of the clock move interminably toward twelve in the indication of nine, and she thought once that she would call him on the telephone, that something might simply have delayed him after all, but she did not believe this, not in the least, and even so small a thing as the call was by now an impossible concession. Still staring at the derisive face of the hall clock, she began to curse him with a kind of cold and venomous clarity, which was the quality and character her anger assumed, and her mind adopted naturally, as if he were there to hear it, the frontal violence of the second person. Afterward, her invective exhausted, she began to think of ways to make him sorry, of all the things that she could do to make him suffer, and she wished and wished with all her heart that he should die. That she should stand and watch and smile as he lay dying.

But this would not be possible, of course, for he was already dead, and had been dead, though she didn't know it, for over an hour.

By nine o'clock, when he was a full hour overdue, longer dead, her anger and shame had grown too great for the house. It filled the rooms and pressed back upon her from the walls, a tangible and noxious density in which she moved with a great effort and breathed with tremendous difficulty. It was quite apparent that she was being slowly smothered, that she must certainly get away from the house at once in order to survive, and so she got a coat from a closet in the hall and went outside.

It was very cold, but she walked with the coat hanging open, and she walked neither fast nor slowly, but with a carefully controlled and imposed gait, as if it were somehow critically important now for the sake of dignity and self-esteem to move and behave in the smallest respects, whether observed or not, precisely as she had always done. Walking in this way, her coat open and her stride measured, she descended the slope from the ridge to the lower level of town, and after a while she came to Main Street and then to the business area and then to the Division Hotel.

Outside the entrance, she became aware that she was cold and tired and desperately in need of a cigarette, and the lobby was suddenly a wonderfully desirable haven that could supply all her needs at once— warmth and smoke and a place to rest. Turning in, she crossed the lobby to the magazine and tobacco counter, and the night clerk, recognizing her, came over at once from the registration desk.

"Good-evening, Miss Haig," he said. "May I help you?"

"I'd like a pack of cigarettes," she said. "Parliaments, please."

He handed her the thin box, and she was reminded then for the first time that she had come off without a purse, and consequently without money.

"I'm sorry," she said. "I seem to have forgotten my purse."

He smiled and made with his shoulders a small gesture of unconcern. "It's quite all right. You can take care of it anytime."

"Oh. Thank you very much."

Standing by the counter, she opened the box and removed a cigarette, leaning forward to accept the light offered by the clerk. Drawing the smoke deeply into her lungs and expelling it slowly, she turned and started back across the lobby toward a cluster of chairs, and then, looking left into the taproom, she saw two young men of some significance in her life sitting at the bar, separated by a vacant stool, and she immediately felt the imperative need of a drink in addition to the needs of warmth and smoke and a place to rest. Changing direction, she went into the taproom and got onto the stool between the two. Her face in the mirror, she noticed, wore a bright and brittle smile, which was rather surprising, for she had not been aware of it, and it was really rather admirable, she thought, to be able to smile so brightly under the circumstances. To rest and warmth and smoke and alcohol was added a final need of flagellation.

"Friends," she said, sustaining the bright smile, "I have been seduced and scorned and left in shame, and I badly need a drink. Who'll buy?"

"I shall," said Ellis Kuder.

"My pleasure," said Guy Butler.

Bernie Huggins supplied it, and the three sat silently side by side in a suggestion of worn expectancy, as if they were waiting for something that might happen or might never happen but must, nevertheless, be waited for.

# THE WITNESS WAS A LADY

It was a Thursday morning when Corey McDown called me. I hadn't heard from Corey for a long time. Not directly. After he got to be a cop, we sort of drifted apart and lost contact with each other. I'm not exactly allergic to cops, you understand, but it usually turns out that we're incompatible.

Corey was a bright guy, and he'd moved up fast in the force. He was pretty young for a lieutenant in Homicide.

"Hello, Mark," he said. "Corey McDown here. Did I get you out of bed?"

"I don't have to get out of bed to answer the phone," I said. "How are you, Corey?"

"I've been worse," he said, "and I've been better. I wonder if you'd do me a favor."

"Do I owe you a favor?"

"Do this one for me, and I'll owe *you* one."

"You think I may need it?"

"You may, Mark. You never know."

"True. There have been times before. What's on your mind, Corey?"

"I hate long telephone conversations. Ask me over."

"Sure, Corey. Come on over."

"Give me thirty minutes."

He hung up, and so did I. It must be a big favor he wanted, I thought, to make him so accommodating. I had an uneasy feeling that it was related to something that I didn't want to think about, and I wished I could quit. I got out of bed and shaved and showered and dressed, which used up the thirty minutes. I had just finished when the door buzzer sounded, and I went out across the living room to the door and opened it.

"Right on time," I said. "Come on in."

He came in and tossed his hat into one chair and sat down in another. His hair was cut short, a thick brown stubble, and he looked trim and hard. Right now, leaning back and smiling, relaxed.

"You've got a nice place, Mark. You live well."

"Heels always live well. It's expected of them."

"You're not a heel, Mark. You're just a reasonably good guy with kinks."

"Thanks." I walked over to a table and lifted a glass. "You want some breakfast?"

"Out of a bottle?"

"Is there another place to get it?"

"I had mine out of a skillet. You go ahead."

I poured a double shot of bourbon and swallowed it fast. Then I went back and threw his hat on the floor and took its place. The double helped me feel as relaxed as he looked.

"Go on," I said. "Convince me."

"Don't rush me. I'm trying to think of the best approach."

"The best is the simplest. You want a favor. Tell me what it is."

"Let me ask you a question first. You seen Nora lately?"

"No. It's been forever. Why?"

"I thought you might have looked her up when Jack Kirby was murdered."

"I didn't."

"That's strange. Old friends and all, I mean. The least an old friend can do when an old friend's boy friend is killed is to offer sympathy and condolences and all that."

"My personal opinion is that congratulations were in order. I didn't think it would be in good taste to offer them."

He looked across at me, shaking his burr head and grinning. The grin got vocal and became a loud laugh.

"You see, Mark? All you've got are a few kinks. A real twenty-four carat heel like Jack Kirby offends your sensibilities."

"Go to hell."

"Sure, sure. Anything to oblige. What I'm leading up to is, this favor isn't really for me at all. Oh, incidentally it is, maybe, but mostly it's a favor for Nora."

"You sound like a man about to be devious, Corey."

"Not me, Mark. Whatever I may be that makes me different from you, I'm not devious. I haven't got the brains for it."

"O.K. Tell me the favor for Nora that's one for you incidentally."

"I'll tell you, but let's get the circumstances in focus. Did you read the news stories about Jack Kirby's murder?"

"Once over, lightly."

"In that case, you'll remember what the evidence indicated. He had an appointment with someone in his apartment. At least someone came to see him there, and this someone, whoever it was, killed him. Cracked his skull with a heavy cut-glass decanter, to be exact. This was all in the news stories, and it's all true. What wasn't in the stories, because we put the lid on it, is that someone pretty definitely knew who it was in the apartment with Kirby that night. That someone is Nora."

"How do you know?"

"Never mind how. We know."

"That won't do, Corey. You can't expect to clam up on the guy you're asking for a favor."

"All right. I'll tell you this much. The day of Kirby's murder, Nora told a friend that she was going to Kirby's apartment that night, but she couldn't go until late because Kirby was expecting someone earlier that she didn't want to meet. This friend is a woman whose testimony can be relied on. We're convinced of that."

"Didn't Nora mention the name of Kirby's expected guest?"

"No. No name. Just that it was someone she didn't want to meet there."

"Did you ask Nora?"

Corey looked down at his hands in his lap. He folded and unfolded the blunt fingers. On his face for a few seconds there was a sour expression as he recalled an experience that he hadn't liked and couldn't forget.

"We hauled her in and asked her over and over for a long while. She wouldn't say. She denied ever having told her friend that she knew."

"I wonder why. You'd think she'd want to help."

"Come off it, Mark. You know why as well as I do. Jack Kirby was a guy who associated with dangerous characters. One of these characters killed him, and he wouldn't think twice about killing a material witness. Either to keep her from talking or in revenge if she did. If he couldn't do it personally, he'd have it done for him. Today or tomorrow or next year. Nora's been associating with some dangerous characters herself, including Kirby. She knows how they operate, Mark. She won't talk because she's afraid."

"Well, Nora's not exactly a strong personality. She'll break eventually. Why don't you ask her again?"

"I wish I could."

"Why can't you? Like you said, she's a material witness. You can arrest her and hold her."

"I could if I could get hold of her." He looked down at his hands again, at the flexing fingers. His face was smooth and hard now, the sour expression dissolved. "I should have held her when I had her, but that was my mistake. A man makes lots of mistakes for old times' sake."

"Asking and giving favors, you mean. That sort of thing."

"Maybe. We'll see."

"Speaking of favors, where do I come in? If you think I know where Nora is, you're wrong."

"That's not the problem. I already know where she is."

"In that case, why don't you pick her up?"

"Because she's across the state line. You may know that we don't have any extradition agreement with our neighbor covering material witnesses."

"I didn't know, as a matter of fact. Thanks for telling me. It may come in handy. I don't seem to remember reading any of this about Nora in the papers."

"I told you. It wasn't there. We've kept the lid on it. The point is, we can't keep the lid on any longer. The story's going to break in the evening editions, and that's what worries me."

"I can see why. You won't look so good, letting a material witness slip away from you. Tough. You expect me to bleed, Corey?"

"It's not that. I'll survive a little criticism. It's Nora I'm worried about."

"Old times' sake again?"

"Call it what you like, but you can see her position. She's a constant and deadly threat to Jack Kirby's killer, whoever he is, and the moment the story breaks, the killer is going to know it. He'll also know where to find her."

"I see what you mean. The threat works two ways."

"That's it. And that's where you come in."

"Don't tell me. You want me to go and talk to her and convince her that she's got to come back and turn herself in for her own good."

"You're a smart guy, Mark. You always were."

"Sure. With kinks. To tell you the truth, I'm not quite convinced that this mysterious visitor of Kirby's is going to be so desperate as you imagine."

"You think he won't? Why?"

"Well, Nora knows he was supposed to be at Kirby's at a certain time. At the time Kirby was killed. So she knows. That's not absolute proof that he was actually there. Even if he was there, it's not proof that he did the killing. It's a lead, Corey, not a conviction."

"A lead's all we need. The visitor killed Kirby. We're certain of it. Once we know who he was, we'll find more evidence fast enough. We'll know what to look for, and how and where to find it."

"You haven't told me yet where Nora is."

"About a hundred miles from here. The first place I thought to check. The natural place for a woman to run when she's scared and in trouble."

"Home?"

"What used to be. Down on the farm."

"Regression, as the psychs say. You were sharp to think of that right off the bat, Corey. You're quite a psych yourself."

He got up suddenly and walked over to a pair of matched windows overlooking a small court in which, below, there was some green stuff growing.

He stood there looking out for a minute or more, and then he turned and walked back but did not sit down again.

"You and Nora were always close, Mark, back there when we were kids. Closer than ever Nora and I were. I used to hate you for that, but it doesn't matter any longer. It's one of the things I've gotten over. The point is, she'll be in danger. I believe that or I wouldn't be here. She wouldn't listen to me, but she might to you. Will you go talk to her?"

"Why should I?"

"Do you have to have the reasons spelled out?"

"I can't think of any."

"As a favor for me?"

"I don't want to obligate you."

"For Nora, then?"

"Nora wants me to leave her alone. She told me so."

"Not even to save her life?"

"Nora's a big girl now. She associates with dangerous characters and makes up her own mind."

He stood looking down at me, his face as bleak and empty as a department store floorwalker's. Turning away, he picked his hat off the floor and held it by the brim in his hands.

"I guess those kinks are bigger than I thought," he said.

He went over to the door and let himself out, and I kept on sitting in the chair, thinking about a time that he'd recalled. She used to ride into town to high school on the school bus, Nora did. Corey and I were town boys. We were snobbish with the country kids until we met Nora, who was a country kid, and then we weren't snobbish any more. She was slim and lovely and seemed to move with incredible grace in a kind of golden haze. She was so lovely, in fact, that she intimidated me for almost a full year before we finally got together on a picnic one Sunday afternoon. After that, I began to know Nora as she was—as a touchable and lusty little manipulator, almost amoral, who already had, even then, certain carefully conceived and directed ideas about what Nora wanted out of life. I didn't love her any the less, maybe more, but I resigned myself to the obvious truth that I was no more at most than a kind of privileged expedient.

After high school, Nora and Corey and I drifted at different times across the hundred miles to the city. At first we saw each other now and then, but later hardly at all. Corey became a cop. Thanks to luck and cards and certain contacts, I learned to live well without excessive effort. As for Nora—well, I had just refused to do her a favor at Corey's request, but there had been plenty of others to do her favors, as there always are with girls like her, and some of the favors came to five figures. Jack Kirby had not been the first. Maybe he would be the last.

I stood up and walked over to the windows and looked down into the court, down at the green stuff growing. I wasn't used to the radiance of day, and the light seemed intensely bright, and it hurt my eyes. My head ached, and I wondered if I could stand another double shot, or even a single, but I decided that I couldn't. Turning away from the windows, I walked back across the living room and into the soft and seductive dusk of the bedroom. I lay down on the unmade bed and tried to think with some kind of orderliness, and the thinking must have been therapeutic, for after a while I lost the headache, or became unaware of it.

Granted, I thought, that Nora knew the identity of Jack Kirby's visitor, who was also Jack Kirby's killer. Corey was convinced that she did, and Corey was a bright guy. Being a bright guy, it was funny how he could go so far wrong from a good start. It was funny, a real scream, but I didn't feel like laughing. Because she'd refused to talk, because she'd run and hid to escape the pressure that would certainly have broken her down, Corey assumed that she was afraid of the consequences of pointing a finger, the vengeance of a killer or a killer's hired hand, but it wasn't true. It couldn't be. She had run from the pressure, true, but she had kept her silence simply because she did not want Jack Kirby's visitor to be known. For old times' sake. It was touching, really, and I appreciated it.

I went over in my mind again with odd detachment, as if I were reviewing an experience of someone else, the way it had happened that I had killed Jack Kirby. I hadn't intended to, although it was a pleasure when I did, and all I'd actually intended when I went up to his apartment that night was to pay an overdue debt of a couple of grand.

I had lost the two grand to Kirby in a stud game that proved to be the beginning of a streak of bad luck. In the first place, to show how bad my luck was beginning to be, I lost the pot on three of a kind, which is pretty difficult to do in straight stud. In the second place, to show how fast bad luck can get worse in a streak, I didn't have the two grand. All I had to offer was an IOU with a twenty-four-hour deadline. The deadline passed, and I still didn't have the two grand. My intentions were good, but my luck kept on being bad. I got three extensions on the deadline, and then

I had a couple of visitors. They came to my apartment about the middle of the afternoon, a few minutes after I'd gotten out of bed. I'd seen both of them around, and I knew the name of one of them, but the names didn't matter. It was a business call, not social. They were very polite in a businesslike way. Only one of them talked.

"Mr. Sanders," he said, "we're representing Mr. Jack Kirby in a little business matter."

"Times have been tough," I said.

"Mr. Kirby appreciates that, but he feels that he's been more than liberal."

"Thank Mr. Kirby for me."

"I'm afraid Mr. Kirby wants more than thanks. He wants to know if you're prepared to settle your obligation."

"How about a payment on account? Ten percent, say."

"Sorry. Mr. Kirby feels that the obligation should be settled in full. He's prepared to extend your time until eight o'clock tomorrow night. He expects you to call at his apartment at that hour with the full amount due and payable."

"Tell Mr. Kirby I'll give the matter my careful attention."

"Mr. Kirby wants us particularly to remind you of the urgency."

"Fine. Consider me reminded."

"Mr. Kirby wants us to remind you in a manner that you will remember." This was the clue to go to work, apparently, for that's what they did. I wasn't very alert yet, it being several hours until dark, and I put up what might be called a sorry defense. In fact, I didn't put up any defense at all. The mute suddenly had me from behind in a combination hammerlock and stranglehold, and the talker, looking apologetic, belted me three times in the belly. At the door, leaving me doubled up on the floor, the talker stopped and looked back, an expression of compassion spreading among the pocks on his flat face.

"Sorry, Mr. Sanders," he said. "Nothing personal, you understand."

I wasn't able to acknowledge the apology with the good grace it deserved. After they were gone, I began to breathe again, and a little later I successfully stood up. The beating had been painful, but not crippling.

It was a break in a way, the beating was. It was the nadir of the streak, the worst of the bad luck, and now that things had got about as bad as they could get, they began immediately to get better. What I mean is, I took the ten percent I'd offered Kirby's hired goons and ran it through another game of stud and brought it out multiplied by twenty. A little better than four grand in paper with not an IOU in the bundle. By midnight I had in my possession, as the talking goon had said, the full amount due and payable.

The next night at eight, I was at Kirby's door. I rang the bell, and Kirby let me in. He was wearing most of a tux, the exception being a maroon smoking jacket with a black satin sash. I happen to have an aversion to satin sashes, on smoking jackets or anything else, and this put me in a bad humor. It made it more difficult than ever to be reasonable about the beating he had bought for me. Apparently I was wearing nothing to which he had a comparable aversion. His long, sallow face, divided under a long nose by a long, thin moustache, was perfectly amiable.

"Hello, Mark," he said. "Glad to see you."

"Even broke?" I said.

"Sorry." His face lost its amiability. "Poverty depresses me."

"Never mind. I'm not one of your huddled masses. I come loaded."

"Good." The amiability was back. "I was sure you could manage if you really tried."

I took the ready bundle from a pocket, two grand exactly, and handed it to him. He transferred it to a pocket of his offending jacket with hardly more than a glance, and this put me in a worse humor than I was already in, which was bad enough. I knew he would count the money the moment I was gone, and it would have been less annoying if he had counted it honestly in front of me.

"Now I'll have the IOU, if you don't mind," I said.

"Certainly, Mark." He took the paper out of the same pocket the money had gone into. "I hope you don't resent the little reminder I was forced to send you."

"Not at all. It was very courteous and regretful, and it only hit me where it doesn't show."

"I'm glad you understand. Will you have a drink before you leave?"

"Bourbon and water."

"Good. I'll have one with you."

He turned and walked over to a liquor cabinet and worked for a minute with a bottle and glasses. "I'm sorry I can't ask you to stay for more than one, but I'm expecting company."

"Company's nice if it's nice company."

"This is nice. Someone you once knew, I believe. Nora Erskine? Charming girl. Beautiful. She has a very warm nature. Very generous."

He came toward me with a glass in each hand, and I hit him in the mouth. Don't ask me why. Maybe a disciple of Freud could tell you, but I can't. He fell backward in a shower of bourbon and came up with a little gun in his hand, which seemed to indicate that he hadn't been quite so amiable and trusting as he'd appeared. The cut-glass decanter was there on a table beside me, and I picked it up and smashed it over his head, and he fell down dying and was dead in less than a minute.

Stripped to the bone, that was how I killed him. I tried to remember if I had touched anything besides the decanter and the outside of the door, and there seemed to be nothing, and so I wiped the neck of the decanter with my handkerchief and retrieved the two grand, which was no good to him, and left. I went home and thought about it, wondering if I should leave town incognito, but I decided that there was no need. The goons knew that I was supposed to be at Kirby's, of course, but the goons were old pros. They'd done a job and were through with it. They couldn't care less that Jack Kirby had got himself killed. As a matter of fact, if they made the logical deduction, I would probably go up immeasurably in their regard. The result of my thinking was the decision that it was unnecessary to take any precipitate action. I only needed to proceed with caution, as the signs beside the highways say, in the direction I was going.

But that was then, and now was different. Now I knew that Nora knew, and Nora was not an old pro, and Nora would surely someday tell. Maybe not now or soon, but someday, the day she couldn't stand the pressure any longer, and the passage of time would not help or save me, for there is no statute of limitations on murder, not even murder which might turn out to be, with luck and a good lawyer, of lesser degree than first. And there was always the solid possibility, of course, of that grim first.

I could see that I had come to the time of decision now, and I didn't want to face it. Like many another in the same predicament, I found a way to avoid it temporarily, if not permanently. In any case it was simple. I simply went to sleep.

When I awoke again, it was evening, but the hour of the day was the only thing that had changed, not me or the problem or anything that had to be considered and done or not done. I got up and washed my face in cold water and put on a tie and jacket and went downstairs onto the street. There was a newsstand on the corner, half a block away, and I went down there and bought an evening edition and carried it back to the apartment without looking at it. In the apartment, I poured another double shot and drank half of it and sat down and opened the newspaper, and there was the story on page one: Material Witness in Kirby Slaying Flees State. I read the story slowly, finishing the second shot of the double as I read, and it was reported about the way Corey had told it to me in the morning, how Nora was believed to know the identity of Kirby's visitor at the time of the murder, and how she had refused to talk, and how, finally, she had escaped into the next state, from which she could not be extradited. It was also reported in the story exactly where she had gone and now was, the home of her childhood not more than a hundred miles away, and this was what I needed in order to make the decision I had to make, and you can see why. Now that her location was no longer a secret shared by me and the police, Nora was in greater danger and, as a consequence, so was I. There was therefore no longer any reason for indecision or delay, although there was probably no reason to hurry either.

I sat there for quite a long while, and it began to get dark outside in the city streets, and the incandescents and fluorescents and neons came on to drive the darkness back. I finally became aware, via my stomach, that I hadn't eaten all day, and that I had better eat something before I took another drink, which I wanted, and so I went out and had a steak in a restaurant down the street a few blocks. After eating, I walked back and had a couple more drinks in the apartment, and then I went down and got my car out of the garage in the basement and drove across town to a place where they were having a stud game. I won five hundred skins in the game, the good streak still running in the wake of the bad streak, and at some point in the time it took to win that much money, my mind made itself up and I knew what I was going to do. I dropped out of the game about three o'clock in the morning, a little after, and it was almost four when I got home.

In the bedroom of the apartment, I changed into slacks, sport shirt and jacket, heavier shoes. From a shelf in the closet I got a leather case that contained a .30-.30 rifle. I had been very good with a rifle when I was younger. There was no reason to believe that I wasn't still almost as good. I assembled the rifle and checked it and took it apart again. I put the parts back into the case and half a dozen cartridges into my jacket pocket. I don't know why I took so many, for chances were long that a dozen would not be enough if one wasn't. Carrying the case, I went back downstairs to my car and drove out of town.

It took me about three hours driving slowly, to reach the town where I had grown up a hundred years or so ago, and I did not drive into it after reaching it. Instead, I drove around it on roads I remembered, and beyond it on another road until I saw ahead of me, quite a distance and on the left, the white house of the Erskines. It sat rather far back from the road at the end of a tree-lined drive, though not so far as memory had it, and it had once been considered the finest farm home in the county, if not the state. Now it did not seem one-half so grand, a different house than I had known before, as if the first had been razed and a second built in its place in an identical design, with identical detail, but on a reduced scale.

I turned off before I reached the house, along the side of a country square. The road descended slowly for a quarter of a mile to a steel and timber bridge across a shallow ravine. There had been water in the ravine in the spring, and there would be water again when the fall rains came, but now the bed was dry except for intermittent shallow pools caught in rock. After crossing the bridge, I pulled off the road on a narrow turning into high weeds and brush. Getting out of the car, carrying the rifle case, I climbed a barbed-wire fence and followed the course of the ravine through a stand of timber, mostly oaks and maples and elms, and across a wide expanse of pasture in which a herd of Holsteins were having breakfast. Pretty soon I left the ravine and cut across two fields at an angle and up a long rise into a grove of walnut trees on the crest. I stopped among the trees and assembled and loaded the rifle, and then I lay down and looked down the slope on the other side of the crest to the house where Nora was supposed to be. There was a stone terrace on this side of the house at the rear. On the terrace was a round table and several brightly striped canvas chairs. Wide glass doors led off the terrace into the house. No one was visible from where I lay under the walnut trees about fifty yards away.

After half an hour, I rolled over onto my back and lay looking up into the branches of the trees where the green walnuts hung, and I began to remember all the times I'd come here to gather the nuts when I was a kid, sometimes with Nora in the later years. We gathered them in burlap bags—gunny sacks, they were called—and later knocked the blackened husks off with a hammer. For a long time afterward, if we didn't wear gloves, our hands were stained with the juice of the husks, a stain like the stain of nicotine, and there was no way to get this stain off except to wear it off, and you could always tell the ones who had gathered walnuts late in the fall by the stain on their hands that wore on toward winter.

I could hear a cow bell jangling back in the pasture. I could hear a dog barking. I could hear the cawing of a crow above the fields, and I thought I could hear, closing my eyes, the slow beating of his black wings against the still air. Opening my eyes, I rolled over and looked down the slope again to the terrace, and there was Nora standing beside the table and looking up toward the walnut grove as if she could see me lying in its shadow. She was wearing a white blouse and brown shorts, and her face and arms and legs were golden in the morning light. Drawing the rifle up along my side into firing position, I had her heart in my sights in a second, and I had a notion that it was a golden heart pumping golden blood.

She must have stood there for a full minute without moving, maybe longer, and then she turned and walked across the terrace and through the glass doors into the house, and I lowered my face slowly into the sweet green grass. I could still hear the bell and the dog and the crow, and I could hear the voice of Corey McDown saying that Mark Sanders was just a guy with kinks.

After a while I stood up and went back across the fields to the ravine and along the ravine through the pasture and the woods to the car. Driving to the city, I thought about what I had better do, and where I had better go, and how long it would take to learn to live comfortably with a constant threat, and I decided, although there was probably no hurry, that I might as well get my affairs in order and get somewhere a long way off as soon as possible.

# THE SPENT DAYS

Cora Rogan came upon the girl at a curve in the walk where a white birch cast a pattern of light shade. She was sitting cross-legged on the grass under the birch, just at the edge of the walk, and shadows of leaves danced with the warm breeze in her hair and on her white dress.

She was playing jacks. She would lean forward and scatter the small metal pieces on the smooth concrete, and then she would toss a rubber ball into the air, letting it bounce once, and between the time it rose and fell and rose on the bounce, she would scoop up some of the jacks, whatever number was required at that particular stage of the game, and catch in the same hand the ball as it descended. She was wonderfully adept at it.

Cora stood and watched her do her twos and threes without a miss.

If she was aware of Cora's presence, she gave no sign.

"Hello," Cora said, after a while. The girl looked up and smiled, holding the jacks and rubber ball in her right hand. She had a small, heart-shaped face with large gray eyes. Although she was very pretty, it was not her prettiness that Cora was struck with, but the serenity in her eyes and smile that seemed to be of a piece with the way she held her hands and head and sat so quietly cross-legged on the grass. "Hello," she said.

"I was watching you play. Do you mind?"

"Not at all. Why should I?"

"I don't know. It might make you nervous and cause you to miss."

"I never get nervous, and I hardly ever miss. Only once in a while, when I get to some of the more difficult things."

"You're quite good, all right. I could see that."

"Would you care to play a game with me?"

"I don't know how."

"Oh, it's very simple. I'll show you as we go along."

"All right, but you mustn't expect me to be much competition." Cora sat down beside the girl in position to use the concrete walk to play on. She could hear someone whistling a tune behind a spiraea bush farther along the walk, but no one was in sight.

"You must throw out the jacks," the girl said, "and pick them up while the ball bounces. Then you must catch the ball in the same hand with the jacks. First you do one at a time, and then two at a time, until finally you must pick them all up together. After that, there are some more difficult things to do."

"Perhaps you'd better explain the more difficult things when we come to them."

"Yes. I thought that would be better. What you must remember is that it's very important how you throw the jacks out. You must try to throw them so that it's easy to pick them up in ones or twos or threes or whatever number."

"I see."

"If you touch a jack you aren't supposed to pick up, or even make it move by pushing another jack against it, that means you miss and must give up your turn."

"All right. I think I understand it up to the more difficult things."

"Then you may have first turn." She handed Cora the ball and jacks, and Cora threw out the jacks and began to play. She went through the ones all right, and through the twos, but she missed on the threes.

"That was very good for a beginning," the girl said.

"Do you think so? Thank you."

"If you had thrown out the threes a little more carefully, you could have gone right on."

"I threw them too hard, I think."

"Yes, they were too scattered for threes. The ball bounced twice before you could pick them up. Did you understand that it's a miss if the ball bounces twice?"

"Yes. I understood that."

"I believe I neglected to tell you."

"That's all right. I knew it."

"Then it's my turn."

She gathered up the jacks and threw them out and began to play and was soon through the game as far as she had explained it. Then she began to do the more difficult plays, explaining each one carefully and clearly before attempting it, so that Cora would know in advance exactly what was required of her.

Some of the plays demanded considerable dexterity, but she completed them all in order, after explanations, and then she laughed with pleasure in her skill, at the same time looking at Cora ruefully because of beating her so easily.

"You're far too good for me," Cora said.

"Well, it's mostly a matter of practice. I shouldn't be surprised if you became quite good after you've played a while."

"I could never become as good as you."

"Would you like to play on through, just to learn? Misses won't count. I'll explain things again as you go along."

"Oh, no. That wouldn't be any fun for you."

"I don't mind. We could play another game after you've practiced."

"No, thank you. I know when I'm thoroughly beaten." Cora laughed and stood up, looking down at the shadows of leaves in pale hair. "I'm on my way up to the house to see your mother. Is she there?"

"Yes. She's on the back terrace, I think."

"Is your father there too?"

"My father's dead. He died before I was born."

"Oh. I'm sorry."

"My mother killed him. She shot him accidentally."

"What a terrible mistake!"

"She told me about it herself when I was old enough to understand. She thought it would be better than having me hear it from someone else."

"Your mother was wise to tell it to you in her own way."

"What do you want to see my mother about?"

"I thought she might like to contribute to a charity I'm interested in."

"Well, I don't know. Mother's very rich, of course, because of all the money Father left her, but she already has certain charities she supports."

"In any case, it will do no harm to ask her, will it?"

"No. You can go right around the house to the terrace if you like."

"I don't think I'd better do that. I'll ring at the front door and ask permission to see her first."

"Perhaps that would be better. Will you be back this way soon?"

"Probably. Pretty soon."

"If I'm still here, I'll say goodbye to you then."

"That would be nice."

"Thank you for playing jacks with me."

"You're quite welcome, I'm sure. The pleasure was mine."

Cora turned away and went on up the curving concrete walk past a small fountain showering water like shards of glittering glass into the sunlight. Beyond the fountain she ascended three wide steps and passed between tall columns onto the veranda of a Colonial-style house.

The house was white with dark green shutters at the windows, and it looked cool and gracious in the white, hot light of the afternoon. It was, in fact, much cooler on the veranda, out of the sun, and Cora waited for a few seconds with the most delicious sense of relief and pleasure before ringing the doorbell.

She was still thinking of the little girl under the white birch beside the walk, and it seemed to her a favorable omen that she had come across her on this particular day.

*It takes Jacks or better to open*, she thought, feeling with the thought the delightful, tremulous sensation of inner laughter.

She rang the doorbell and waited, listening to the sounds of diminishing chimes, and soon the door was opened by a woman in the uniform of a maid. Conditioned air, escaping, flowed outward.

"Yes?" the maid said.

"I would like to see Mrs. Morrow," Cora said.

"Who shall I say is calling?"

"Cora Rogan."

"Will you state the nature of your visit, please?"

"It's personal. If Mrs. Morrow will be so kind as to see me, I'll take only a few minutes of her time."

"If you'll step in and wait a minute, I'll speak with Mrs. Morrow."

Cora stepped into a wide hall which divided ahead of her, ascending spirally on the right to the second floor and running on the left through the house to the rear.

The maid closed the front door and walked down the hall past the staircase, turning and disappearing into a room on the right side, and Cora remained standing in the cool, conditioned air. Her reflection waited with her, trapped in glass on a wall beside her, and she exchanged long looks with the reflection and smiled a little and was, on the whole, rather pleased.

She was thirty-eight now, no longer young, but she was slender as a girl in a beige linen suit, and her flesh was still firm, with only the slightest deepening of lines around the eyes and mouth, and she could still pass in soft light for what she really no longer was. Nowadays she grew tired more often than she had used to, of course, and once in a while she became a little frightened when she thought of the years that had gone so swiftly and the years that had still, somehow, to come and go.

Turning away from the reflection of herself, she looked slowly around the hall, her eyes moving deliberately from one thing to another, and she thought as she looked that it was much the same as it used to be. There was a new runner on the stairs, and the telephone on the table against the wall was pale green instead of black, and the painting on the wall above the telephone was different from the one that had hung there before—but nothing of any significance had changed, not even the basic colors or the subtle sense of character that houses have.

She took a couple of steps toward the stairs, her thin heels tapping sharply on the gleaming hardwood floor, and at that moment the maid reappeared suddenly in the hall at the rear and came forward.

"If you will come this way, please," she said, "Mrs. Morrow will see you."

Cora followed her down the hall and off to the right into a large room with high, wide windows and a pair of glass doors opening onto a flagstone terrace. The maid stopped just inside the room and nodded toward the doors, through which Cora could see, sitting in a bright canvas chair beside a glass-topped table, a woman in a sheer flowered dress. On the table were an open book, lying face down, and a pitcher and matching glasses.

Cora crossed to the glass doors and let herself out onto the terrace, and the woman, Julia Morrow, stood up beside the table and greeted her with an expression in which there was the slightest suggestion of curiosity.

"Good afternoon, Miss Rogan," she said. "Will you sit down?"

"Thank you," Cora said. "It's kind of you to see me."

It was clear, she thought, that her name meant nothing to Julia Morrow, for there was no evidence of recognition in the tone of her voice, nor even the careful kind of control one might exercise to exclude such evidence.

Moving across the flagstones to the glass-topped table, Cora sat down in a bright chair, and Julia Morrow resumed the one from which she had just risen. The chairs were not placed directly opposite each other across the table, only a small arc of the circumference separating the two women. Their relative positions seemed to indicate a condition of intimacy, as if they had drawn together to exchange confidences.

"May I offer you some iced tea?" Julia Morrow said.

"No, thank you."

"Then what can I do for you?"

"To tell the truth, it's rather difficult to begin. I see that you don't recognize my name."

"You name? Cora Rogan? I'm sorry. Should I recognize it?"

"Perhaps not. I was our husband's first wife."

Now the expression of curiosity, wholly confined to Julia Morrow's eyes, gave way for an instant to a flare of surprise. It was gone, however, almost before it was discernible, and afterward there was no expression except courteous reserve.

"I see. I knew that my husband's first wife was named Cora, of course, but I had forgotten the rest of it. I understood that you had remarried."

"So I had, but it pleases me to use my maiden name. I lived with my second husband in Europe. He's dead now."

"I'm sorry."

"It was no great loss. We lived well, one way and another, but he left next to nothing. It's apparent that you have done much better."

"I have all that I need. Have you come to see me simply because we shared, at different times, the same man?"

"It occurred to me that I didn't offer my sympathy at the time of his death. I thought I should come and do so."

"After all this time? It was eight years ago—nearly nine."

"So long as that? Time goes, doesn't it? Or is it we? Someone wrote a poem about that once. About its being we who go instead of time. Was it Ronsard?"

"I don't know. I read very little poetry."

"It must have been terrible for you. To kill your own husband by mistake, I mean."

"Yes. It was terrible."

"As I recall, you thought he was a prowler. You shot him with a shotgun, I believe, as he was coming up the stairs. The light on the stairs, I remember, had gone out for some reason."

"There was a prowler scare in the neighborhood. James had left the shotgun, loaded, in our room. I wasn't expecting him home that night, and I was terrified. The recollection is painful, however, and I'd rather not discuss it."

"Forgive me. The inquest, of course, was quite brief. Hardly more than a formality. You had, it seemed, absolutely no motive for killing your husband intentionally. Besides, your condition at the time solicited a great deal of sympathy."

"I was expecting a child, if that's what you mean."

"Yes. Your daughter. A charming little girl. I met her beside the walk as I came up to the house. We played a game of jacks."

"She's rather casual with strangers. It disturbs me sometimes."

"I envy you. I have no child of my own, even after two marriages. I remember how astonished I was when I first learned that you were going to have one."

"Really? I wonder why."

"I was, as I said, your husband's first wife." Cora smiled gently and looked away for a few moments with an air of abstraction, as if the remembrance were pleasant, although a little sad. "It was quite impossible for him to have children."

Julia Morrow was also suddenly withdrawn. Only a faint expression of fastidious distaste indicated that she had heard the words and understood their implication.

"That's absurd," she said. "Are you suggesting that James was mutilated like that foolish character in the Hemingway novel?"

"Nothing so romantic." Cora laughed softly and returned her gaze to the woman across the arc of glass. "To use your own term, it was really rather absurd. A kind of bad joke. Orchitis is the name for it. A complication of mumps." She laughed again, softly, with a note of genuine amusement. "It was terribly humiliating to a man as vain as poor James. You don't object to my calling him James, do you? It made him a comic character in his own eyes, and he wouldn't have dreamed of confiding in anyone about his misfortune. At the time of his death, his doctor having died before him, I rather imagine no one alive was aware of it except three people. You and me, Mrs. Morrow, and James himself. I wonder, if it had been generally known, how it would have affected the inquest—in the matter of motive, I mean. It's an interesting speculation, isn't it?"

"Not particularly." Julia Morrow's voice, under perfect control, was the vocal equivalent of her fastidious expression. "I find it boring, as well as absurd. However, allowing the motive, I should think it would have worked in reverse. The wrong person was killed."

"It might seem so, superficially. However, you must admit that we are in the position of *knowing* who was killed and who was not." Cora was silent for a few seconds, seeming to consider what she had said, and then she spoke again casually. "Tell me, Mrs. Morrow, why *did* you kill him? Was he going to divorce you? But of course he was. He was so vain, poor dear, that he could never have tolerated infidelity in his wife, even at the price of publicizing his own inadequacy. Under the circumstances, it would have been a disaster, wouldn't it? You would have received nothing, of course. As it is, you now have all that you need, haven't you?"

"You twist my words against me." Julia spoke and then was still. If she was shocked or greatly concerned, she didn't show it. After a while she sighed. "What do you want, Cora Rogan? Surely you realize that it would be extremely difficult to establish anything against me after so long a time."

"It's hard to tell." Cora reflected and shrugged. "Who knows what would happen if it were all to be revived? At the worst, ruin. At the best, a great deal of unpleasantness. Especially, it seems to me, for the charming little girl I met on my way to the house. Did I tell you that we played a game of jacks?" Julia Morrow rose abruptly and moved a few steps away. She stood for a minute staring across the sunlit yard to a row of Russian olive trees at the rear, silvery-green in the light, and then she turned and came back to the table; but did not sit down again.

Cora smiled secretively.

"Why have you waited so long?" Julia Morrow said.

"I am not an avaricious person," Cora said. "Until recently I lived well and had no need. Now I'm in need."

"Tell me what you want"

"What do I want?" Cora spoke dreamily, like a child with an impossible wish. "I think, more than anything else, I should like to return to Europe and live the rest of my life there. I know of a small villa in the south of France where I could live quite cheaply. For one who is clever in making the best of things, fifty thousand dollars should be quite sufficient for me—for a long, long time."

"For the rest of one's life, I should think."

"Yes. For the rest of one's life." Julia Morrow sat down. She closed her eyes, apparently tired, but her face was composed.

"Are you sure I can't offer you some tea before you go?" she said.

"Quite sure." It was Cora Rogan's time to stand. "I've intruded long enough."

"Are you staying nearby?"

"At the hotel in town."

"How uncomfortable for you. The accommodations are deplorable, I understand, but of course there are very few guests in such a small place. You probably won't want to stay long."

"I hope to leave tomorrow afternoon. I'm expecting a small package before then."

"I'm sure you won't be disappointed."

"You're very kind and thank you again for seeing me."

Cora left without looking back; but she did not go, as she had come, through the house. She walked around the outside along a walk bordering beds of bright flowers, and so past the fountain and around the concrete curve to the white birch and the little girl.

"Did you see Mother?"

"Yes. We had a nice talk."

"Did she give you something for your charity?"

"She's thinking about it. I'm sure she will."

"I'm glad. Would you like to play another game of jacks?"

"No, thank you. I really must go."

"All right. I guess I had better go back to the house now, anyway. Goodbye."

Cora watched her go up the walk alone. For a few yards she walked sedately, and then she broke suddenly into the gait that seems peculiar to small girls—something between a trot and a skip, or perhaps a little of both by turns.

Standing under the white birch and staring after her, Cora had suddenly so intense and terrible a sense of loss and loneliness that she cried softly aloud, unaware, in anguish. In that instant the small villa in the south of France was a far and empty place of exile, and she envied the vulnerable woman she had just left on the terrace—the woman who had saved something, as Cora had not, from the sterile years.

The girl had gone away and left her jacks in a little pile on the grass beside the walk. Bending down, Cora picked up the small metal pieces and dropped them into a pocket of her linen jacket.

She would keep them, she thought, as a memento of this day—and all the spent days before.

www.ingramcontent.com/pod-product-compliance
Lightning Source LLC
Chambersburg PA
CBHW050759250626
47155CB00005B/2135